DAUGHTERS OF THE MOON

the talisman

LYNNE EWING

HYPERION/NEW YORK

Volo® is a registered trademark of Disney Enterprises, Inc.
The Volo colophon is a trademark of Disney Enterprises, Inc.

First Edition
3 5 7 9 10 8 6 4 2
Printed in the United States of America

Library of Congress Cataloging-in-Publication Data on file

ISBN 0-7868-1878-6

Visit www.volobooks.com

To Lynn Waggoner and Barbara Fullerton—
puellae convivii semper *(party girls forever)!*

Maggie stood on the roof of her apartment building, her eyes weak and unable to bring the night lights into clear focus. An ocean breeze curled around her back, and the sudden chill roused a sharp pain in her spine. She had waited too long to take the potion given to her when she was a girl in Athens.

Now she pulled the glass vial from her skirt pocket and held it to the eastern sky. The liquid inside shimmered silver, anticipating the moon. For the potion to work best, she had to drink it in moonlight. But sometimes she took it during the day, finding pleasure in the stunned expressions of the people who witnessed her transformation back to youth.

A sad smile crossed her wrinkled face, mirroring her mixed emotions. It was time for another to take her place. She would have to tell her successor soon.

In her own mind it was clear. When evil forces in the world became too strong, the good in the universe always sent someone to restore harmony. Saints, mystics, sometimes a prophet, once a savior. This time an ancient moon goddess had come to earth, but as often happened, she had no awareness of her true identity. The girl was hostile and filled with too much self-confidence. What would she do when she learned the truth? It had been nearly impossible to convince her that she was a Daughter of the Moon, and now Maggie had to tell her that she was an ancient goddess and destined to take Maggie's place.

At last the moon rose. Its gentle radiance touched the flask, and the potion became a rainbow of lights spiking from the glass. Maggie sipped the sweet elixir. Heat seared through her veins, and a delicate pain prickled through muscle, bone, and skin. Her body tightened, becoming young again.

When she finished drinking, the flask vanished, leaving only a cascade of sparks in her thin, graceful hands. This was the end. She had no potion left to restore life. That was sad but good. After living for more than two thousand years, she was ready.

Her mind turned back to the girl. How would it feel to think you were one person and then learn you were entirely another? Convincing the girl was not going to be an easy task, but it had to be done quickly.

A sudden change in the wind jarred her thoughts. Her stomach twisted as fear rose inside her. The gust blew from the northeast. Such winds always carried omens of doom. She traced her fingers through the humming currents, gathering the vibrations on the tips of her fingers. She breathed it in and knew with terrible certainty that the Atrox had somehow escaped her binding. It had taken human form again, but how was that possible?

She turned and hurried back to her apartment, praying she wouldn't be too late this time. As she rushed down the stairs, memories of her youth came flooding back.

CHAPTER ONE

431 B.C.

PENELOPE STOLE through the streets of Athens, her pale, moon-colored hair flowing behind her. Thick smoke from the sacrifice of a hundred sheep and oxen during the day still hung in the air. She stopped and peered around the corner into the next alleyway. She had to be careful. Her father would be angry if he discovered she had gone out alone again at night, and her punishment would be severe this time.

She walked quickly now, her fingers tracing over the dusty walls, and began to shiver even though it was windless and warm. Fear of men far crueler and more dangerous than her father filled her with an internal cold that penetrated to her bones.

Most Athenians believed the gods controlled their fate, but Penelope had felt the dark presence of another, even greater force. That was why she had defied her father and gone to the secret ritual in the temple of Selene. Only those who had been initiated into the mysteries of the moon could take part in the ceremony, but she hoped soon to be invited to join their rites.

Men's laughter echoed down the passageway. She hid and for the first time in her life felt grateful to be so short and small. She squeezed behind a twisted olive tree growing in a narrow opening between two houses.

Four soldiers walked past her, unaware of her presence, the smell of sweet wine flowing around them. One fanned his hand through the glossy leaves overhead, and a spray of gray-green olives fell on her.

She waited until their footsteps had faded, then slipped from her hiding place and started home again. Her father was a powerful commander in the Athenian navy. Like too many Athenians, he dreamed of a Greece united into one state under Athens. The navy had already attacked several other city-states, forcing them to join the Athenian empire, and now Sparta had declared war on Athens.

She started across the agora, her thin leather sandals slapping against her heels. The temporary stalls were empty, but the smells of turnips, roses, olives, and myrtle berries still lingered from the day. Huge administrative buildings surrounded the market on all four sides, but now the distant columns and corridors were silent and filled with dangerous shadows where something evil could have hidden.

She bounded down a long line of stairs, wanting nothing more than to be home, but as she passed the springhouse where the women and slaves gathered each morning to draw water, she became aware of other footsteps. She darted inside the small building and dipped her hands into the cool water, then wiped her face, trying to wash away her fears.

After she had waited long enough for the other person to pass, she started to leave, but odd muffled voices made her stop. She pressed back into the darkness and held her breath, listening. Beneath the sound of gurgling water came low, eager whispers trying hard not to be heard.

She peered out at the night. In the distance a dim orange glow lit the moon shadows, and before long, a lone soldier turned from a corridor, carrying a torch. The flame flapped lazily and made shadows twist over the walls beside him.

He staggered forward, drunk, holding his torch fire high, but it was the dark behind him that held her attention now. Shadows intertwined and rolled over each other as if preparing for some purpose. A slice of shade slipped over the man's shoulder and clung to his cloak.

Then, as mysteriously as the phantom forms had appeared, they vanished. She blinked. The soldier's shadow was the only one beneath his feet now and hulking like a giant on the wall beside him.

Maybe her eyes had deceived her. She started

to leave the springhouse again, but before she could, the dreamlike silhouettes returned, swelling behind the soldier. He stopped midstep and tilted his head, as if sensing something.

Abruptly he swirled around, whipping his torch like a sword. The flame cut through the thick gloom, and an eager keening came from the dark as if his attack had somehow roused it.

Then a man taller than the soldier stepped from a nearby stretch of cloudy shadows. The fold of his cloak was pulled over his head, making a hood that hid his face. He grasped the soldier's shoulder, his fingers long and white.

The soldier cried out and turned, thrusting his torch out in defense. The flame must have burned the man, but he didn't flinch or even step back.

"Sorry," the soldier said in greeting, a smile forming on his face. "You startled me."

But his friendly grin soon fell away. He dropped the torch and thrust his hand back, fingers grasping the hilt of his sword, but before he could draw the blade, other men appeared from the dark and crowded around him.

The tall man pushed back his hood, revealing thick black hair. It glimmered in the light cast by the fallen torch as if the sun were shining on it. In rising horror, Penelope realized that he burned with some internal flame.

Her chest tightened with fear and her stomach knotted. She ignored the little voice inside her telling her to escape and instead stayed. Some morbid curiosity made her strain and twist her head to watch.

The soldier's eyes filled with wide-eyed terror.

"Run," she whispered, but he looked too afraid to flee.

He started to scream, but the sound fell from his mouth in a faint whistle as if something dreadful in the tall man's face had silenced him. Then his chin dropped again, and this time a deafening shriek filled the air.

She rested her cheek against the cold marble. Her body trembled violently. The cry seemed to echo inside her, a death song.

The soldier's lips remained parted and a

thick white mist wreathed his mouth. She watched, both fascinated and repelled, as the men surrounding him nudged hungrily closer, like a gathering of starved wolves, breathing in the vapor.

Slowly, the men turned and started walking away with lazy footsteps, their faces serene, as if some desperate need had been satisfied. The soldier ambled after them, his cloak dragging on the ground, feet unsure, but not from wine now. It was as if the others had stolen his life and he was dead, but walking.

The tallest one turned, his stillness frightening, and seemed to look directly where Penelope hid in the darkness. His eyes flashed yellow. She ducked back, closing her eyes against what she had seen, but after a moment's hesitation made herself look out again as if some force were compelling her.

Whatever the man had been now spun into the darkness like a plume of smoke. Then it was gone. A heavy and unbearable quiet returned, and except for the gurgling of the spring waters and her own jagged breathing, it was as if the world had stopped.

She shuddered, feeling a terrible guilt descend upon her. Nausea overcame her. She should have helped the soldier, but what could she have done except become a victim herself?

She turned around and plunged her hands into the cold water behind her, then held them against her cheeks, desperately trying to calm her churning stomach. The sound of her retching would bring them running back.

"Never again," she whispered, and stopped at the sound of her own ragged voice.

She waited a long time, afraid to leave her hiding place. She had seen men like these once before, when she and her sister had strayed away from a nocturnal festival. She had sensed then that they were different from other people, but when she had asked her father about them, he had only laughed at her girlish imagination and scolded her for straying from her chaperones.

But her slave, Nana, had believed her. Even now Penelope remembered the frightened look on

Nana's pale freckled face when she told her about the people with the strange, staring eyes of slavish devotion.

Nana had said they were Followers, who worshiped an ancient power called the Atrox, a force dedicated to destroying the good in the world. But she had refused to say more. Instead, she had sent Penelope to the temple of Selene for her answers.

Penelope wanted those answers, and at the same time she did not understand her own determination. She had no proof, and when she had asked Pandia, her mentor at the temple, she had been frustratingly vague in her answers. What had she witnessed tonight? She needed to speak with Pandia again, and soon.

Abruptly the normal night sounds returned. An owl screeched. Crickets and cicadas chirped. Somewhere a dog howled.

She darted from the springhouse, the air warm and natural against her skin. She didn't care who might see her now.

Faded moonlight and lingering smoke filled

the streets with a twilight gloom, and the hazy gray darkness made her uneasy. She glanced up. Normally the acropolis could be seen from anyplace in Athens, but the overhanging haze now eclipsed it and its invisibility frightened her. She quickened her pace, her lungs burning, and studied the shadows for any unnatural movement.

At last she opened the front gate to her home and walked down a corridor to the courtyard. Men's laughter and music from a kithara and flute came from deep within the house. Maybe her father was still entertaining and wouldn't notice her return. She was about to step onto the mosaic floor under the portico when rough hands grabbed her shoulders.

She let out a startled cry.

CHAPTER TWO

PENELOPE TURNED and bowed her head, ready to face her father. "I'm sorry," she said.

"Why?" The heavy hands fell away. "Thank you for waking me."

She looked up. Nicias, her father's night watchman, rubbed his eyes, then stretched his fat arms. She must have nudged him when she opened the gate.

"Your father would have been angry if he had caught me sleeping again." He brushed his fingers through his white beard. "Especially with the men leaving tomorrow."

Penelope felt the gratitude in his voice. She wasn't the only one who feared her father's anger.

"I'm glad I found you," she lied.

"I'd better get back." Nicias turned slowly and ambled toward the gate.

Penelope had started into the house again when a shadow slipped around the altar in the center of the courtyard and streaked toward her. Her muscles tensed and she took in a sharp breath, waiting.

Then her fourteen-year-old sister, Taemestra, flashed from the dark into the light cast from a line of clay lamps and ran to her, the hem of her linen tunic wrapping around her thin ankles.

"Where have you been?" Taemestra asked. Gold earrings dangled against her neck, and the perfume of roses wafted from her luxuriant hair. "I've been waiting half the night for you."

Penelope glanced back at Nicias, hoping he hadn't heard. He was sitting at the gate, his head already nodding in sleep.

"I had a few errands." Penelope shrugged, trying to avoid her sister's questions.

"You're supposed to send slaves to do errands." Taemestra offered her a bite of the honeycomb she held pinched in her hand and tilted her head with a sly look. "Where were you really?"

"I told you." Penelope bit into the wax and savored the thick sweetness in her mouth. She didn't sense any threat that Taemestra would tell their father. Still, she wondered why her sister had waited up for her. She seemed almost frantic with energy.

"I was afraid you weren't going to get home in time," Taemestra said, taking back the honeycomb.

"For what?" Penelope asked. Maybe her father had been looking for her after all.

"In time to see the treasures father brought home." Taemestra grabbed her wrist, then looked at her oddly. "Why are you so cold? The night's warm."

"I saw the people again," Penelope confided, finally saying what she had wanted to share with someone.

"What people?"

"The ones we saw that night."

"Is that where you've been?" Taemestra frowned.

"I saw them turn into shadows." Penelope quickly told her sister everything she had seen.

When she finished, Taemestra looked skeptical. "Why do you always imagine more than you see?" She repeated the question their father had often asked.

Penelope felt a flash of anger. "Can you explain what I saw?"

"They were probably wall diggers," Taemestra answered.

Penelope paused. She hadn't considered that. The exterior mud-brick walls in many of the homes in Athens were so thin that, instead of breaking in through a door or window, burglars would dig a hole through the wall to rob a house of its treasures. The practice was so common that people had begun calling burglars "wall diggers."

"It's possible, I suppose," Penelope said at last.

"Of course, that's it." Taemestra pulled her inside.

Flames from oil lamps flickered around them, and in the shimmering glow the dolphins in the frescoes seemed to leap in serpentine arcs over the curling blue waves.

"The smoke from the sacrifices is still heavy," Taemestra continued. "And robbers going back and forth through a hole in the wall would create an illusion of men disappearing into shadow and re-forming again."

"But the soldier—" Penelope started.

Taemestra waved her hand through the air as if she were batting at a bothersome fly. "If he had stumbled into a group of thieves, then maybe the tall one stabbed him and he staggered after them, hoping to find help."

Penelope nodded, hating her cowardice even more now. "I should have stayed and helped him," she whispered. "But I felt so frightened."

"Your fear is the easiest to explain." Taemestra ate the last of the honeycomb.

"It is? How?" Penelope was beginning to

doubt everything that had happened. In the solid comfort of her home it was difficult to believe she had felt such terror.

Taemestra spit out the glob of wax into her palm and tossed it back in the courtyard. "You were terrified our father would discover that you'd gone out again."

Penelope took a deep breath, feeling suddenly foolish. "Maybe you're right."

"Of course I'm right." Taemestra smiled. "Now come with me." She grabbed Penelope's wrist, her fingers sticky with honey, and pulled her past the slaves' rooms toward the north side of the courtyard, heading for the men's quarter.

Penelope knew where she was going and stopped. "We can't go in there. Only men are allowed in the *andron*."

"No one ever told us we couldn't peek in." Taemestra tugged harder, her eyes filled with mischief. "Besides, the men are having a symposium. They'll never even notice us."

Penelope relished the idea of spying on them. "I wish they'd let us go to their drinking parties." She breathed in the strong fragrance of wine and olives coming from the back of the house and the last remnants of her fear vanished, replaced with excitement; she wanted to see who her father was entertaining.

Music and laughter became louder as they tiptoed over the black-and-white pebble mosaics in the anteroom. Now that they were this close, it was impossible to turn back.

Penelope's heart raced and her hands trembled as she braced herself against the wall and peered inside the main entertaining room. Wicks burned in oil pots set on tripods, the light flickering across the brightly painted yellow wall. Three men lounged with the girls' father, each on his own dining couch.

Finger bowls were placed on small tables in front of them next to plates of cheese, onions, olives, and figs. The fish had already been eaten, and the bones lay scattered about the floor. Two black dogs lay impatiently waiting for more scraps.

Her father's favorite slave, Annyla, a pale

woman with blue eyes from Thrace, ladled out a thick soup made from beans and lentils. The steam curled into her thin face as she handed each man a bowl.

In the corner three musicians played flutes and a kithara, the music sweet and haunting.

Penelope watched, her stomach quivering with the thrill of spying on the men. Or maybe the heady feeling came from doing something forbidden. "Who are they?"

"Soldiers who are going to sea with Father," Taemestra answered. "I cornered Annyla in the kitchen and made her tell me what she knew. They can't be that old, sixteen or seventeen at most."

"And far too beautiful to waste on war." Penelope was bewitched by the one nearest the far wall. Excitement rushed through her as she wondered what it would feel like to talk to him alone.

"Father says it will be an easy victory over Sparta." Taemestra seemed confident.

Penelope didn't feel as sure. "Already the Spartans have burned our crops and we have to live behind the city walls."

"You worry too much," Taemestra assured her. "Our fleet will bring back grain and everything else we need."

"I hope." Penelope peeked back into the andron.

The musicians started another piece, and this time the men sang along.

"They're as handsome as the gods on Olympus," Penelope said, more to herself than Taemestra.

Taemestra turned to look at her. "It's not like you to be swayed by the beauty of men. Maybe you'll fall in love with a mortal and marry after all."

"Maybe." Penelope pulled back, her mood suddenly somber. She loved her younger sister, and even though they were only a year apart, she had tried to protect her and care for her after their mother had disappeared, but she hated the way Taemestra believed the rumors that Penelope was actually a daughter of Zeus.

Now she stared at Taemestra's pale skin and glossy black hair pulled back in a stylish bun at the nape of her long neck. Were they really full sisters? Their coloring was different. Penelope was short and small. Taemestra was tall, graceful, and already looked like an elegant woman.

All her life Penelope had heard whispers about Zeus's amorous misadventure with her mother. Could Zeus be her true father? Surely if he were, she would have felt the wrath of Hera, Zeus's first wife, before now? But Hera's anger could also account for their mother's disappearance. No one knew if she had deserted them or if something more sinister had happened to her.

For the longest time Penelope had imagined her mother ill and needing her daughter's care, but when the days turned into months, darker thoughts intruded, and she envisioned her mother, who had always been so kind to her slaves, now a slave herself, a prisoner of some Persian warlord, forced to dance and sing to entertain men. Even now she shuddered, imagining her mother's hair cut short, her arm and neck marked with the tattoos of a slave.

Eventually, she had decided her mother must have been dead, because she had loved them too much not to find a way to return if she had been alive. Now Penelope bit her lip to stop the ache in her heart and wished she could see her mother one last time. That morning her mother had left the house as if it were an ordinary day, not their last moment together.

"I adore the soldier with the dark hair." Taemestra interrupted Penelope's thoughts, pulling her back to the present. "I hope to marry him."

"You can't just marry him." Penelope was sometimes astounded by Taemestra's audacity. She followed her sister's gaze and assumed she was talking about the man on the middle couch, who was looking at them now. He did have radiant hair and deep eyes, a good face and powerful arms. "Father has to negotiate your marriage."

"I'll have him," Taemestra said, as if it were already settled.

"You'll end up with some old man like everyone else," Penelope teased.

Taemestra shook her head. "Not me. I'm going to marry for love."

"That's nonsense," Penelope warned. "No one does. Besides, how can you love him when you don't even know him? He could be married already."

Taemestra played with a tendril of hair that had fallen from her bun. "I'll find out. It's better to love than to accept an arranged marriage."

Abruptly, their father held up his hand and the musicians stopped playing. He swung his legs to the side of his couch.

At once the men washed their hands in the finger bowls, then wiped them on scraps of bread and tossed the leftover chunks to the dogs.

Slaves gathered the sandals and began tying them on the men's feet.

Penelope jerked back her head and stumbled, bumping into Taemestra. "They're getting ready to leave."

Holding hands, they bounded toward the courtyard, the skirts of their chitons swirling around their legs.

"Daughters." Their father's voice boomed behind them.

They stopped and turned slowly.

Taemestra groaned. "He's going to be furious."

"I told you we shouldn't have spied on them." Penelope looked up, her heart racing.

"Would you like to meet my friends?" their father asked. Another time he would have scolded them, but his eyes looked merry now, the way they once had before their mother had left.

"I think Dionysus has sweetened his temper," Penelope whispered.

He walked into the courtyard, swaying slightly, his smile broadening. Annyla followed close beside him to catch him if he stumbled. The young men came after him, the smell of wine heavy on their breath.

"Yes, Father." Taemestra stood straighter, her fingers smoothing down her tunic as if she enjoyed being on display. "If it pleases you, we'd like to meet your friends."

"This is Milon," their father said with a wink.

A young man who still didn't have a beard stepped forward, holding his helmet in the crook of his arm.

"Milon." Taemestra repeated his name, acting as if she had never seen a man in their home before. Her eyes seemed almost hungry.

Penelope felt embarrassed by her sister's forward behavior, but Milon looked captivated by her. Perhaps Taemestra was right. Maybe she could choose her husband.

"And Hector," their father added.

Hector didn't bother to conceal the way he was looking at Penelope. She returned his gaze, admiring his square chin and the black curly hair that fell into his eyes. He was much taller than their father and seemed twice as broad. She wanted to run her fingers over the hard muscles in his arms. She blushed. Where had such a thought come from? She looked away, afraid of what her hands might do if she continued to stare at his incredibly handsome face.

"And this is Eteocles."

A blond man stepped toward them. He

already carried a long, lashing scar from a battle across his cheek.

Taemestra nodded and smiled up at him as if he were a god. "I've seen you throw the javelin," she whispered.

Penelope blushed for her sister; men practiced athletics naked. How had Taemestra seen?

When she glanced back at Hector, his eyes were fixed on Taemestra; he seemed infatuated with her beauty. Penelope frowned. This wasn't the first time a man had looked away from her to admire her sister, but it was the first time her chest had filled with fiery jealousy.

She clenched her jaw and stared down, kicking with the tip of her sandal at a mosaic of a fish. A tiny black stone from the eye came free and skipped across the floor. She looked up, hoping no one had seen, and slipped her foot back under her tunic.

"Good night, Alcibiades." Hector said and clasped their father's arm. "And thank you."

Penelope stared at him, wishing she could think of something to say before he left. She wanted to know him more, even though that was impossible unless her father agreed.

Hector swirled his cloak over his shoulders, and the tip of the linen brushed through her hair. It aroused a strange desire within her. His eyes caught her gaze. Embarrassed, she looked away.

Taemestra said good-bye, her voice sweet like a song, as the men walked across the courtyard.

"Good night," Penelope joined in. She didn't want Hector to leave without giving him something to remember her. "May the immortal gods bless your journey." The words croaked out and her father turned, his stare warning her to silence. She blushed, unable to control her tongue. "And may bright-eyed Athena guide you."

The men looked at her curiously.

Her father gave her a thunderous look.

Suddenly, her own foolishness seemed unbearable, and she ran from the courtyard. Her feet clattered up the stairs, and when she was in the safety of her room, she slammed the heavy wooden door behind her.

Why had she acted like such a child? It all

just proved she needed to seclude herself and dedicate her life to Selene. She chewed on the inside of her mouth, trying to control an irresistible urge to have one last look at Hector. What had caused such an impulse? She had never felt this way about a man.

She picked up her lyre, surprised by the trembling in her fingers, and sat down to play. She plucked at the strings, trying to banish the pictures of Hector from her mind, but a sudden memory of his eyes on hers filled her with yearning.

Her fingers fell from the strings, and for no reason that she understood, she began to cry, the tears coming from deep inside her. She wished her mother were there to explain these new and confusing emotions to her.

CHAPTER THREE

PENELOPE AWAKENED with a start. A piercing ray of sunlight blinded her. She leaned back in her bed and shaded her eyes. She rested her head against the wall, then remembered what day it was. Abruptly she swung her feet to the floor, fearful that her father might have left already. She grabbed a simple cloth band, wrapped it around her chest, then dressed in the linen tunic with the geometric pattern on the border.

As she started to pull her hair into a bun, securing it with ribbons, a sudden sense of foreboding shot through her. She wasn't sure if it was the remnant of a dream or if she had caught a glimpse of the future, but panic seized her. The Spartans were savage fighters, and even though her father planned only to attack from the sea, that didn't mean he was safe. She had to stop him from going.

She hurried from her bedroom, her bare feet thumping heavily on the wooden stairs.

Her father stood alone in the courtyard near the altar, his eyes locked on the small statue of Athena. A breeze ruffled through his long gray hair and beard as if the goddess's fingers were caressing him.

"I don't want you to go." Penelope fell against him, savoring his warmth.

He squeezed her into his huge arms, then released her, his eyes distant, as if in his mind he were still sending prayers to the goddess of war.

She tried to coil her worries back inside her, but the ominous feeling only became stronger. Her heart felt on fire.

"We shouldn't be at war with Sparta," she said, "but uniting with them to fight the true enemy."

"And that is?" He seemed almost curious now. That gave her hope he might listen.

"The ancient force that causes war," she answered.

"Men and the immortal gods make war," he said sternly.

"But there is another power that wants to destroy all good," she insisted.

He looked sad and weary. "I shouldn't have let Nana remain in this house after your mother disappeared. She's too superstitious and has filled your mind with irrational ideas."

"It's not Nana," Penelope answered, searching for the right words to convince him to stay.

He smiled, his eyes showing the pride he held for her. "But your stubbornness comes from me."

Her father was giving her the opportunity to end the discussion so they could have a peaceful good-bye, but she couldn't suppress the need to keep him safe at home.

"Please," she continued. "You don't understand." She started to say more, but sudden laughter made her turn.

Hector, Milon, and Eteocles stood in the courtyard behind her. She hadn't heard them enter. What had she done now? Even Hector was smiling and saying something to his friends, seemingly about her. Her chest felt hollow.

"You think we're not fighting the right enemy?" Hector looked strong and rugged in the kilt of leather strips, decorated with ornately etched metal plates, that hung to his knees. Bronze covered his broad chest and caught the sun's rays.

"I wasn't aware you were listening," she said boldly, wondering how long they had been standing there. She hoped they mistook her blush for heat from the day.

"We couldn't help but hear," Milon answered.

"As long as you have heard my feelings, then you should also know that I hate the way men say that war is needed for the sake of the city's women." She couldn't seem to stop the words pouring from her mouth.

"We are defending you," Milon spoke back, his eyes narrowed with impatience. "Why else would we go to war?"

"You aren't fighting for me." She glared defiantly at the disapproval on their faces. "If I had my way, you would—"

"I caution you to be quiet now," her father interrupted. "Your words are treason."

"But—"

"Enough." He clapped his hand over her mouth and pulled her back into a dark storeroom. The smells of onions, garlic, wine, and barley meal were heavy in the cool air.

"I will not allow you to speak to me that way and make me look weak in the eyes of my men." He was obviously furious, but kept his voice low.

She folded her arms over her chest, then dropped them to her sides, defeated. "I only wanted to keep you from going into battle. I never meant to shame you or dishonor you."

"I must lead the men into battle," he told her. "Their lives are in my hands, and I need to know that I can count on them."

"I'm sorry," she whispered. "It's just that I awoke with a strong feeling that it was too dangerous for you to go."

"The gods control our fate." He raised an eyebrow, daring her to contradict him.

"It's unwise to disregard unfavorable omens." She glanced up, hoping that her remark might persuade him.

But he scowled. "Only soothsayers and priestesses can see the future. You've become too much like Nana. Soon you'll be throwing curse tablets and burying lead dolls with the dead."

Then he smiled tenderly. "How am I ever going to arrange a marriage for you if you behave this way?"

She shot him a stormy look. "I plan to dedicate my life to Selene."

His voice hardened again. "You'll marry when I say you'll marry."

"I can't accept such a limited life." Her father didn't interrupt her defiance this time. Maybe he sensed the tears brimming in her eyes.

"Women are restricted," she continued. "And confined to the house. I want the same freedom that men have."

"You'll have children," he offered, and the

kindness in his voice made a tear tremble and spill down her cheek. "I'll arrange a fine marriage for you."

"Yes." She bowed her head, but her mind and body rebelled against the future her father saw for her.

He touched her cheek, the huge calluses from his sword scratching against her skin. "I have to leave now."

She clasped his hand and held it there. The terrible feeling of foreboding overcame her again and made her tremble.

"My going away has always frightened you," he said. "You're afraid of losing me the way you lost your mother, but I promise I'll come home to you."

"May the gods make it so," she whispered.

"Will you say the libation over the wine for me?" he asked.

She nodded even though her stomach tightened in pain, terrified that this would be their last morning together as father and daughter.

CHAPTER FOUR

OUTSIDE THE courtyard the call of sad good-byes joined marching footsteps. Dust billowed in soft clouds, rising above the wall, as men left for war. Penelope waited near the altar, breathing in the smell of spicy wine from the jug clasped in her hands. A bee buzzed lazily over the family's offerings of almonds, honey, and figs set around the statue of Athena.

Taemestra leaned against Penelope, her eyebrows fixed in a scowl.

Hector, Eteocles, and Milon stood beside Penelope's father. Slaves and servants hovered nearby.

"I'm sorry for my outburst," Penelope

said at last. "I didn't mean to offend anyone."

Her eyes shifted carefully to her father. He nodded, pleased with her apology, then held up the empty phiale, indicating that the ceremony might begin.

Penelope poured wine into the shallow bowl. When it was full, she spilled more on the ground, an offering to the gods to ensure that they would be on her father's side during the battle. But even as the purple drops stained the stone slab, she imagined the mothers and daughters in Sparta making similar offerings. How could the gods decide whom to favor?

Her father took the first drink from the phiale, then handed the bowl to Eteocles. He sipped, his eyes closed as if concentrating on his prayers. Then Milon drank. At last it was Hector's turn. He took a long swallow.

When Hector handed the bowl to Penelope, her fingers brushed against his. The touch sent a sweet thrill through her. She gazed into his eyes, startled. He looked away quickly, as if upset. Did he think her too bold?

Uncertain, she sipped the spicy wine.

She turned to give the last drink to Taemestra. Her sister took the bowl and shot Penelope a bitter look. Was her downcast mood another act for the men, or had something more than their departure upset her? She was obviously unhappy, but about what?

When the bowl was empty, Penelope stood back and extended both her arms. She brought her hands together, palms open, and prayed, invoking the gods, trying to enlist their support for the Athenian navy.

Her petition ended and she looked at their father. "May Athena guide you into battle and Zeus give you protection." Then she pulled the sleeve of her tunic over her head to veil her face in a gesture of modesty, devotion, and loyalty. She could feel her sister beside her doing the same.

Silently the men picked up their helmets, shields, and iron swords. They walked toward the gate, their footsteps heavy and determined, each seeming to contemplate the journey ahead.

Hector turned, a sadness in his eyes. Was he sorry to be leaving?

Taemestra stepped boldly forward and grabbed their father's arm. "I'm going to walk a little way with you."

Their father didn't deny her request.

She left and walked with the men down the dust-filled corridor to the waiting cart that would take the girls' father to the harbor and the fleet. She carried her father's helmet, the black-and-white horsehair crest brushing against the bottom of her chin.

Penelope waited at the gate, afraid she wouldn't be able to hold back her tears.

At the corner, her father held Taemestra protectively, then took the helmet and slipped it on his head.

Hector turned, and even from a distance Penelope knew he was staring at her. She felt the comfort of his gaze on her body. Her eyes held his, with longing for him. He was the last one to turn the corner, and then he was gone. She understood her sadness in seeing her father go off to war, but why did she feel such grief for Hector? Was this the emotion Taemestra called love?

CHAPTER FIVE

TAEMESTRA RAN back to the house, the wind tousling her black curls, her tunic snapping around her legs.

Penelope licked at the salty tears that had gathered on her lips and brushed the wetness from her cheeks, then held her arms open to comfort her sister as she always had.

But Taemestra didn't crumple against her and cry. She shoved past her, barged through the gate, and collapsed on a bench in the courtyard. "Your insolent manner and rude talk are chasing all the men away," she said.

"What are you saying?" Penelope walked over to the bench, the sun hot on her shoulders.

Taemestra folded her arms over her chest, looked away, and stared at her toes. "Why do you think Father hasn't been able to find anyone to marry you?"

The question surprised Penelope. She had never considered why she wasn't pledged to anyone. She hadn't been interested in marriage and had assumed that was the reason their father was taking his time. "Has Father been trying to find someone for me?"

"Everyone knows he can't find anyone for you, no matter how much he offers for your dowry." Taemestra lifted her head and glared at Penelope, disbelief in her eyes. "Don't pretend you didn't know."

"I didn't." Penelope sat down on the bench.

"If you're not concerned for yourself, could you at least stop being so antagonistic until after I'm married?" Taemestra's rage broke into jagged sobs, and when she spoke again, her words were hopelessly mingled with heaves and sniffles. "I'm fourteen years old, and most girls my age are married or promised to someone. Some even have babies already."

"What does my behavior have to do with you?" Penelope touched her arm, trying to soothe her. "Surely men know the difference between a wife and her sister. Besides, I don't think anyone could ever chase a man away from you."

The hint of a smile crossed Taemestra's lips and then dissolved into a frown. "They're going off to die for us, and you said such horrible things to them, as if you think their deaths are no sacrifice at all."

"I apologized—" Penelope started.

"It's your angry words they'll remember," Taemestra interrupted.

"I didn't mean . . ." Penelope's words trailed off, and her sadness transformed into something worse, bringing new tears to her eyes. "I was just trying to open their eyes to other possibilities."

"Do you think you're Socrates?" Taemestra smiled unhappily, as if picturing Penelope wandering the streets of Athens like a beggar and discussing philosophy with anyone who would listen to her. "I'll disown you if you think something like that. It's enough the way you continue to humiliate me and Father the way you do."

Penelope stared at the sky. Seagulls soared in ever-widening circles. She wanted to escape the conversation and join them. "I don't mean to dishonor anyone."

"You've changed so much in the last year." The criticism rushed from Taemestra's mouth as if she had been waiting a long time to say it. "It's as if you're trying to ruin our family."

"I have changed," Penelope whispered.

"But why? We were so happy before. Everything was perfect."

Penelope glanced at Taemestra, her mind rushing to the thought of their mother's disappearance. "Perfect?" She didn't bother to hide the accusation in her question.

"We were as happy as could be expected without our mother," Taemestra corrected herself, but her tone was angry. Maybe Taemestra blamed their mother for leaving them.

"Mother would have come back if she could have," Penelope said. "Something happened to her, or she'd be with us still."

"But now I'm losing you." Taemestra's chin started to quiver again.

"Me?" The accusation startled Penelope. "I'm here for you. Even now I am trying to comfort you."

"You're not the same." Taemestra shook her head, her earrings catching the sun and reflecting shards of light. "You weren't this serious and suspicious even after Mother left. What changed you?"

Penelope took a breath. "Don't you remember the people who chased us that night at the festival a year back?" She felt baffled, wondering again why her sister didn't share the memory.

Taemestra let out a long sigh. "We were having fun. That's what I remember, too much wine and freedom."

Penelope shot a look at her sister, her own frustration rising. "How can our memory of that night be so different?"

"Everyone was frolicking," Taemestra explained.

Penelope touched Taemestra's shoulder as she had that night. "How can you not remember the terror we felt?"

Taemestra caught her gaze and shrugged. "If you saw me shivering, then it was from cold, not fear. Maybe the wine didn't agree with you."

"The man grabbed you," Penelope continued sharply. "And you screamed."

"With delight." Taemestra laughed. "He was trying to steal a kiss, and I wish now I had let him, because unless you stop chasing the men away, that's probably as close as I'll ever come to having anyone kiss me." She looked sideways at Penelope.

"His eyes glimmered yellow in the moon-light," Penelope said, wondering if she had imagined it all.

"No, they didn't." Taemestra slapped at her, playful now, her way of apologizing for her earlier anger.

Penelope leaned her head against the wall. "I wish I had the answers."

"To what?" Taemestra asked.

"I want to know why I remember it so

differently than you." The sunshine became suddenly too blinding and warm. Penelope cupped her hands over her brow, shielding her eyes.

"It's because you have too much imagination." Taemestra raked both hands through her thick hair and yawned. "It must be both your curse and your gift from the gods. Isn't that the way it is? A gift always comes with a curse."

"Maybe we should go to the oracle," Penelope suggested, still troubled. "She could tell us what has happened."

"To my memories?" Taemestra's head snapped around and Penelope caught something in her eyes. Then it was gone.

"At least we'd know what happened that night," Penelope said.

"I'll go with you, but not to ask such a foolish question." Taemestra adjusted the bracelets on her slender arms.

"What would you ask, then?" Penelope wanted to know.

"Who I'm going to marry, of course." Taemestra grinned and settled back, a dreamy expression on her face, as if she were imagining a husband someday.

Penelope sighed.

Taemestra shot to her feet, her sweet smile back. "Come on. Everyone's going to the acropolis tonight to make offerings. Let's have Annyla braid our hair so everyone will look at us with envy."

"I'll join you in a minute."

Taemestra hurried across the courtyard and disappeared into the shadows behind the marble columns.

Penelope stayed on the bench, rubbing her temples. Her father and Taemestra insisted that she had too much imagination. Could that be it? Then an idea came to her. Her mentor, Pandia, had always been evasive in her answers, but now Penelope decided to find her before the day was over and demand some resolution. She couldn't face another night without knowing the truth.

CHAPTER SIX

PENELOPE HAD BEEN unable to find Pandia, but now she hoped to see her at the acropolis. She shifted her basket of sweet cakes and wine to her hip and started walking on the crowded ramp leading up the steep rocky hill. Flickering flames from clay lamps and torch fires lit the path with a golden glow. Owls nesting on the slopes added their soft, haunting cries to the murmur of conversation flowing around her.

By the time Penelope had reached the spacious stairs leading into the propylaea at the top of the slope, she had caught the excitement and energy of the people jostling around her. Poor, foreign, and slave women were seen on the streets and in the marketplace, but she rarely saw the wealthy, aristocratic women outside their homes. Now they climbed the steps, their flowery perfumes spinning into the balmy night air. Gold and purple threads woven into their fine clothing seemed to shimmer and caress their bodies.

Some had darkened their eyebrows with lamp soot; others had painted their lips and covered their faces with white lead, their cheeks with rouge. Slaves trailed behind them, hair cropped short, carrying lamps, wooden paddle fans, and baskets filled with offerings for Athena.

Penelope stepped into the gateway. It was built of white marble with a magnificent roof high overhead. She made her way past the columns, then climbed five more steps and reached the rear porch. She stepped out and looked up.

The great bronze statue of Athena towered above her; its gleaming metal caught the firelight and cast it back. Her father said the statue could be seen from several miles out at sea.

Penelope merged with the crowd meandering around the statue, then made her way past the large heap of ashes, charred wood, and bones, remnants from offerings of the day before. Sacrifices had also been offered on the Areopagus across from the acropolis, and in front of the small temple of Athena Nike. The burnt smell lingered in the air.

She climbed the steps to the Parthenon and looked out across the city, past the burned fields to the moon's reflection on the sea. She wondered if Hector was now staring out at the same water.

When she turned back, she caught a glimpse of Pandia. The cloth of her tunic was woven with such skill that her clothes clung to her and flowed around her body. Her skin was the palest white, her eyes bold. Silver bracelets twisted around her delicate wrists and her matching earrings and necklace shimmered, seeming to light her black, luscious hair.

Pandia no longer went out during the day, preferring the beauty of the night, and rumors had circulated that she bathed only under the moon's glow. Those who had seen her claimed that something magical happened when she stepped into the pool of water inside the temple. No one discussed her age, but Penelope sensed that she was as ancient as the gods.

Two older wealthy women dropped their veils and glared at Pandia. Penelope wondered if they felt such scorn because Pandia had come to the temple unchaperoned, but then with a jolt realized that she had done the same. Taemestra always brought a retinue with her, to show off her status, but Penelope detested the way rich women flaunted their position with troupes of slaves.

"Pandia!" Penelope shouted.

The stunned matrons looked at her, disapproval and contempt on their faces.

Pandia turned and their eyes locked.

"Wait," Penelope called, but Pandia ignored her and slid behind a pillar.

Penelope pressed through the women standing in groups and tried to catch up to Pandia, but the crowd became too dense, and she lost her.

Slowly she climbed the steps on the west side of the Parthenon and entered the temple through its massive doors. Her arms and elbows brushed against others in line with her, heading down the broad central aisle. The gold-and-ivory statue of Athena rose high above her, and at once she was overcome with reverence and awe.

Persian helmets and Spartan shields captured in past battles leaned against the pedestal in thick stacks, some spilling out onto the floor among the offerings circling the giant statue of the powerful goddess. The smells of incense, flowers, wine, sweet honeyed cakes, old leather, and rusted iron rushed around Penelope. She breathed deeply and squeezed her offering between an iron sword and a pile of spears, then stood back and gazed up into Athena's face.

"Bright-eyed Athena," she began, calling the goddess to gain her attention. Her voice joined those of a hundred others, offering prayers and hoping to invoke the power of Athena to protect their loved ones. The petitions rose in a pleasant chant and echoed through the colonnaded temple. But even as Penelope was swept away by the sweet resonance of the many voices praying together, she wondered why she felt so much concern for Hector.

More worshipers surged around her, and reluctantly she left to make room for others waiting at the door.

Outside, women had gathered on the steps in small groups, whispering and pointing. Penelope followed their looks. Pandia stood with three elderly men too bent with age to go off to war. It looked as if Pandia were arguing fiercely with them. She never shied away from men the way women were taught to do. She approached them fearlessly and spoke openly. Penelope admired her candor, but the well-bred women standing nearby with their slaves studied her with ire.

"She's conceited and brash." Taemestra was suddenly beside Penelope, whispering in her ear. "That's why her father was never able to negotiate a marriage for her."

"Maybe she didn't want one," Penelope said, defending her.

Taemestra snorted, as if the idea were ridiculous. "All women want to marry, but look at how old she is. No one will ever want her."

Penelope sighed. "Maybe she's dedicated her life to other things."

"Like what?" Taemestra looked bewildered.

Penelope wanted to tell her sister what she herself planned to do, but before she could speak, Taemestra grabbed her wrist, pulling her toward the gateway. "It's a good thing I found you."

"Why?" Penelope asked, trying not to lose sight of Pandia in the throng.

"What were you thinking to come here unescorted?" Taemestra smiled at a wealthy matron whose slave was fanning her with a wooden paddle. "Someone could have seen you and told Father."

"I think your real concern is what people might say about you if they see your sister here alone." Penelope tried to pull away from her.

Taemestra frowned. "You should act in accordance with your position." She motioned to Nana and Annyla. "We had better go now."

"I need to speak to Pandia first." Penelope slipped away from Taemestra and squeezed through the crowd. She caught sight of Pandia again and called her name. "Pandia!"

Pandia glanced back, but gave no sign of recognizing Penelope. She continued walking down past the outer colonnade of the Parthenon, her steps quicker now.

Penelope eased through the crowd, shoving when she had to, but when she reached the east side of the temple, Pandia was gone.

"Penelope." Taemestra ran after her, her eyes fiery with anger. "You're embarrassing me."

"Go on," Penelope ordered, catching sight of Pandia near the propylaea.

"I will not." Taemestra spoke in a low voice and glanced around at the women staring at them now. "Please, not tonight. Not here. Behave properly . . . for me."

"I'm sorry." Penelope jerked away and bounded toward the gateway. She ran through it, moving sideways at times, then headed down the ramp, bumping and nudging through the steady stream of women coming up the hill to the acropolis.

When she reached the bottom, the crowd had thinned. Pandia stood alone, pausing to wrap her cloak around her.

"Pandia!" Penelope shouted. There was no chance Pandia couldn't have heard her call, but she acted as if she hadn't and started walking again.

Penelope stopped to catch her breath. Her heart thudded with disappointment. How could she have been so foolish? Her constant questioning had obviously become an annoyance to Pandia, and now Pandia was avoiding her. She should have waited until she had been invited to partake in the mysteries of the moon before asking her questions, but as always, she had become too impatient.

Now she wondered if Pandia had decided Penelope wasn't worthy of joining Selene's sacred cult. Maybe she planned to tell her so the next time they met at the temple. But if that was the case, then Penelope was determined to hear it now. She wasn't going to have her failure announced in front of the other novitiates.

She charged after Pandia, sprinting down the long, dusty road, then turned onto a narrow street. The skirt of her tunic tangled hopelessly with her legs, but she didn't slow her pace. When she came to a crossroads, she stopped. She could no longer see Pandia, but she could still hear the steady slapping of her sandals against her heels. Recklessly she followed the sound of her foot-steps.

A mist began to roll in from the ocean, glinting silver in the sky; then its tendrils drifted to the ground, winding around trees and homes, at last dropping to the ground and muffling all noise.

Penelope turned another corner and found herself at a dead end in front of a potter's shop. The smell of damp clay filled the moist air. She quickly retraced her steps, but now all sound was gone and there was nothing left to guide her.

Defeated, she started home, laboring to catch her breath. She had only gone a little way when she sensed a change in light and glanced up. The foggy gray shadows had taken on a curious glow of fire. Bobbing orange globes increased in number until at last she realized that a torchlight procession was marching toward her.

Soon the street was lit, and even though the faces of the marchers were covered by their cloaks, she was certain that some of the men in the procession were the same ones she had seen the night before.

A chill raced up her spine, and her stomach tightened. She slipped into a dark alley and crouched low, her muscles tense, ready to run as soon as the men passed, but the march broke apart without warning, as if by some silent command. She sensed intuitively that they were searching for her even though she didn't understand why. What would they want with her?

The air became still, pressure mounting. She didn't see anyone, but she had the curious sensation that invisible hands were pressing her forward. Her heart lurched, and she looked behind her.

When she did, a voice rustled across her mind. She drew in a sharp breath. How was that possible? A whisper lolled over her thoughts, clearer this time. Someone was calling her and telling her to join the procession.

She blinked, trying to clear her head, but the furtive command came again, stronger now. She was overcome with an irresistible need to follow the voice inside her head. She stepped forward, and a shock of fear raced through her. She grabbed a nearby column, pressing her cheek against the cool marble, trying to calm herself and resist the mad impulse.

She shuddered, and then the night seemed to close around her, the darkness becoming opaque and deep. At once she felt the air pull at her as if she were in the ocean and an undertow were sucking her out to sea. She fought against it, not understanding what it was, but then something cold and bitter spread through her and she lost her will. Her hands fell to her sides and she started walking toward the licking flames of the torches held by the few from the procession who had remained on the street.

But as she stepped into the moonlight, the silver glow struck her eyes and her head snapped back. If she had been in a trance, it was gone now. She shook her head, feeling a strange dizziness, and wondered what had drawn her forward. She slipped back into the shadows, hiding between stacks of baskets that smelled unpleasantly of fish.

A strip of moonlight shone on her back, giving her comfort. She glanced up at the moon, then quickly scanned the dark behind her, suddenly remembering the odd way the shadows had shifted and formed behind the soldier.

She crouched lower, staying within the serenity of the moonglow, then peered back at the street. A swath of darkness slithered over the wall, blacker than the misty shade. She pressed her cold, trembling fingers against her eyes, hoping it was only a trick of vision, but when she looked up again, the shadow was closer, winding over the street and into an olive tree as if searching for something.

Her breath caught, and in her nervousness her elbow slipped and knocked into a stack of baskets beside her. She winced. Even that small snap of reeds had been too loud. She looked up in panic, certain she had been heard.

The wrinkle of darkness stopped suddenly, as if sensing the air; then it changed direction, coming directly at her, streaking through the night, a sleek black snake gliding toward her with terrible speed.

She bolted to her feet and bounded away, only to stumble into another pile of baskets. She tripped and fell. Her chin hit the ground, and the vile presence of something corroded and old stirred in the dark around her. She could taste its foulness on her tongue, and even though she saw nothing in the dark with her, she could feel it crawling over her skin.

She tried to drag herself away, but it was commanding her to turn. She could feel the pull of its will, becoming stronger than her own.

Something touched her shoulder and she let out a startled scream, then froze. She was too frightened to turn and see what stood behind her.

CHAPTER SEVEN

"**B**E SILENT," A voice whispered behind Penelope. Delicate hands grasped her arm, the fingers impossibly long and beautiful in the moonlight. Whoever it was helped her stand, and the spell broke apart.

Penelope turned.

Pandia stood behind her, seeming more goddess than woman, sheathed in a soft aura of moonlight.

"Thank you." Penelope tried to meet Pandia's gaze but looked away, feeling embarrassed and ashamed. Her weakness had been revealed to her mentor, and now she would never become part of the mysteries of the moon.

"We'll go to the temple of Selene," Pandia said brusquely. "If something happens to me, you must continue on yourself. Selene will guide you."

Suddenly Pandia clutched Penelope's wrist, pulled her back, and stood in front of her.

Lazy shadows lolled beneath an olive tree. The glossy leaves fluttered as the darkness underneath pulled together, becoming thick and solid, fusing into a tall man. When the transformation was complete, the man stepped from the dark and started walking toward them with slow, easy steps.

Penelope gasped. It was the man she had seen with the soldier.

His eyes flashed open. He looked at her, taking his time, as if she belonged to him. Black threads of shadow seeped from his body, wreathing toward her with unspeakable menace.

She started to scream, but before she could, Pandia traced her hand through the air. Sparks trailed after her fingers like shooting stars, forming a shield.

The man stopped, but other somber shadows gathered around him, rising and falling in deepening layers of gloom. Their soft wails filled the night with a keening like the voices of starved wolves circling prey.

Pandia stood defiantly still, as if she were challenging the man. Penelope had the odd sense that they were communicating in some way; then the spell broke, and Pandia grabbed Penelope's hand and yanked her around.

"Quickly!" she yelled, already running.

They ran through the darkness, feet smacking the ground, tunics whipping about them. But the shadows were faster, screaming across their path and swimming beneath their feet. One tethered Penelope's ankle. She tripped and stumbled forward. It slithered up her leg to her spine, its cold seeping deep into her flesh. At last it settled around her neck, strangling tight. Her lungs locked.

"Pandia." She choked, struggling to breathe.

But even before she had fallen, Pandia had started turning, as if some preternatural sense had made her aware of the danger. She wrested the shadow from Penelope's neck and flung it away. It twirled into the milky fog, forming the shape of a thin man. With catlike agility he landed on his feet, turned, and started walking toward them, his face lean, eyes flaring yellow.

"You fear the light." Pandia smirked and lifted her arm, stretching it out as if she were going to caress his cheek. A white luster curled around her fingers, starlight shimmering on the tips.

The man paused, then twisted and turned, trying to escape backward, but before he could dissolve, a silver light streaked from Pandia's hand.

The man raged, then gyrated and disappeared in a plume of smoke.

"Hurry." Pandia nudged Penelope forward.

The stealthy darkness ran with them until they burst into an open field near the temple. Silver moonlight washed over them.

Penelope turned her head, feeling safer now, and slowed her pace. The shadows remained in the narrow street between the houses, calling her back with whispery voices. Vapory black tendrils darted out from the shade, only to retreat from the moon's glow.

At last they ran up the ramp to the temple, slipped from their sandals, and stepped into the sanctuary. They stood in front of the sculpture of Selene driving her moon chariot with six ferocious white horses. A fire burned near the statue in a giant marble disk. Flames danced and were reflected in the horses' eyes, bestowing them with life.

Overhead a window pierced the roof, showing a breathtaking view of the night sky. The stars shone clear, and the moon's radiance gleamed across the marble floor.

"Come with me," Pandia urged, already heading away, her tunic sweeping behind her.

At the back of the temple, Pandia lit a small oil lamp and started down a narrow stairway. The small flame flickered, making their shadows jump across the craggy wall.

Penelope watched warily, unable to make her

breath come in an even rhythm, the stone steps cold beneath her feet. Her body began shaking violently, but she didn't think it was from the chill in the air.

At last they reached a secret chamber cut deep into the slope of the hill. Pandia hurried about the room, lighting lamps suspended from wall brackets. When she was finished, she guided Penelope to a chair with a curving back and armrests decorated with inlaid ivory designs. She wrapped a blanket around Penelope's shoulders, and then her fingers glided over Penelope's cheeks as if seeking reassurance that she hadn't been harmed. A comforting warmth grew inside Penelope, giving her the peculiar feeling that Pandia's touch was penetrating deeper than bone, searching for injury of her spirit.

Pandia left then, and when she returned, she carried a small vessel of honeyed wine, her bare feet silent on the marble floor.

"It's better if fewer people know of your plan to pledge your life to Selene." Pandia sat down on a stool and set the wine and cups on a three-legged table. "I ignored you at the acropolis because I thought it was best for us not be seen in public together."

"Why?" Penelope wondered. Was she such an embarrassment to their sect? Maybe others would have fought the shadows instead of cowering the way she had.

"There are forces trying to stop you before you make your commitment to Selene." She poured wine into a cup and handed it to Penelope. "I don't want them to see us together, because they will know your time is approaching soon."

Penelope held the cup tightly between both hands, hoping to stop her trembling fingers. Still, the wine swished back and forth, almost spilling. She took a quick swallow, then set the cup aside. The sweetened wine burned her throat but didn't ease the knot in her stomach. The safe life in which she had been reared was slipping away from her. "What forces?" she asked at last, hating the tremor in her voice.

"The same people who stole the crescent moonstone from the temple," Pandia continued.

"The oracle has said disaster will follow if the stone is not returned to its rightful place."

"Maybe a robber has taken it," Penelope offered.

"Only a fierce power could have lifted it from its setting," Pandia went on. "That's why Selene has given me permission to tell you about the Atrox."

Penelope felt dizzy and knew it wasn't from the wine.

"During the primordial chaos that existed before creation, the Atrox breathed life into itself and strove to be the first ruler of the universe."

"How could it give itself life?" Penelope asked.

"Even great Zeus doesn't know the answer— only that it did." She went on. "Gaia and Chaos fought its evil force. They created Tartarus deep within the earth and imprisoned it there. Tartarus was strong enough to hold the Cyclopes and the Giants, but it couldn't keep the Atrox contained."

Penelope pulled the blanket tighter, but she didn't think anything could ever ease the chill running through her.

Pandia continued, "The ancient gods created another land beneath the dark clouds of Tartarus, but the Atrox now uses that realm for its shelter and freely roams the world above and in between, and its Followers are growing in number."

"The people . . ." Penelope thought a moment. "The shadows we saw tonight."

Pandia nodded. "The Atrox and its Followers want to destroy all good. I fear that even the great goddess Selene won't be able to contain the evils still held within the bottom of the world if the Atrox is not stopped."

"What evils?"

"The ones that never escaped Pandora's box," Pandia answered. "Moon legend says a young woman of pure and brave heart will unlock the door that imprisons those evils and release the next storm of disease and suffering."

"If it's locked, it must take a key to open it, and such a woman would never unlock—" A strange idea gripped Penelope. "Why are you telling me?"

"Because a key that can unlock the door can

also be used to lock it," Pandia answered simply. "The moonstone sacred to Selene is the key. That's why it was guarded here, in her temple."

"But why tell me?" Penelope asked, her heart hammering.

"You wouldn't be told these things if you weren't meant to know." Pandia removed a chain of woven gold and silver from around her neck and clutched an engraved amulet hanging from it. She handed it to Penelope.

Penelope held the talisman. An odd vibration came from the stone, as if its power were straining to be released. She started to read the incantation inscribed on it, but Pandia's hand closed her lips.

"You must never speak the words," she warned. "Their power is too great."

"But if I must never say the words, then why were they etched into the stone?" she asked, her frustration rising.

Pandia stared at her, her eyes reflecting the oil-lamp flames, and something more. "Reciting the chant would consume you."

"What if someone else accidentally finds it and reads it?" She thought of Taemestra and her unstoppable curiosity.

"Only you can see the words. The letters won't reveal themselves to anyone but you . . . until it's time to pass on the amulet. She will be able to read the words."

"She?" Penelope slipped the chain around her neck; the talisman jiggled against her chest, then settled.

"That's when you'll know you have the rightful successor." Pandia paused. "She'll be able to read—"

"A successor to what? What am I supposed to do?" Penelope was possessed with growing belief that Pandia must be speaking to the wrong person.

"The oracle has seen the future," Pandia answered, sensing her doubt. "It's best if you take your vows soon, so that all secrets can be revealed to you."

Penelope started to agree, but then an image of Hector filled her mind. "I need to see Hector one last time before I do." The words were out before she was even aware she had spoken them.

Pandia gazed at her, but there was no surprise on her face. Had the oracle also envisioned Penelope's hesitation? "You can see Hector when he returns, but for tonight you must remain hidden in the temple. Your destiny will begin to unfold soon, and I need to keep you safe until then." Her words lingered in the air with a sense of foreboding.

CHAPTER EIGHT

THE NEXT DAY, as Penelope crossed the courtyard in her home, she heard the steady rhythm of weaving coming from the *gynaikeion*. She climbed the stairs, the wood creaking beneath her feet, and stood in the entrance to the private rooms used only by the women. Fine wool fibers and dust floated in the air over baskets of green, blue, and red yarns.

Annyla sat in a corner, feet propped on a footstool, her hands picking dirt, twigs, and bits of leaves from the matted raw wool on her lap.

Taemestra stood in front of a vertical loom,

tossing the shuttle back and forth across the threads. Her head turned. "Penelope!"

Taemestra dropped her shuttle and ran to Penelope, throwing her arms around her and squeezing her. "How could you scare me like that? I thought you had disappeared like Mother."

Annyla and Nana pushed Taemestra aside and hugged Penelope, kissing her fiercely.

"All night." Taemestra scolded her again. "You shouldn't have stayed away that long without getting word to me. I was worried to death."

Nana appeared distressed, her eyes swollen, lids red, as if she had spent the night crying. Even Annyla had the worn look of someone who had gone without sleep, but Penelope didn't sense her sister's anguish. She looked well rested.

"Where have you been?" Taemestra repeated.

"The temple," Penelope answered honestly.

Nana shook her head as if she didn't approve and went back to her work. She took a wooden rod covered with raw wool in her left hand, then drew out a few strands with her right, twisted them into a thick thread, and tied them to the spindle. The weight on the end spun, twisting and pulling the strands into yarn. More fibers drifted into the air.

"You could have sent a messenger." Taemestra seemed angry now, but there was more pout than frown on her face. "You're all right. That's all that matters."

Taemestra pulled Penelope over to the loom. "Tell me everything." She picked up her shuttle. The steady beat of the heddle rod moving the threads up and down started again.

Nana hovered over Taemestra, obviously annoyed with her work. Nana had the hopeless task of improving their weaving skills.

"Nana, I need to speak with you," Penelope said quietly. She had loved to hear Nana's stories about her nomadic life in the land north of the Black Sea before she had become a slave, but now she had only one question.

Taemestra snapped her head around, eager to hear, but before Penelope could speak, Nana cautioned her with a nod, her eyes motioning Penelope away from Taemestra.

Penelope followed Nana to a far corner of the room. She had always had the impression that Nana didn't like Taemestra. Now she wondered why.

Nana picked up her spindle and began twisting the raw fibers into yarn.

"What do you know about the Followers of the Atrox?" Penelope asked.

"To speak of them is to bring them closer." Nana stopped spinning and looked behind her, her old eyes studying the dim corners of the room.

"I saw them again, and I need to know more about them. It's important."

Nana bit through the thread she had been twining. Tiny wisps of wool clung to her cracked lips. "It's ill fortune to talk about these people. They can sense when words are whispered about them, and it brings them forth."

"But I need to know," Penelope repeated.

Nana shook her head. "I told you to go to the temple of Selene."

"I did, but they didn't tell me what I need to

know." She lifted the amulet. "My mentor gave me this, but warned me never to use it."

Nana took in a sharp breath.

"I hear the men have won an easy victory over Sparta," Taemestra said suddenly.

"How do you know that?" Penelope asked, wondering if Taemestra had purposefully interrupted their conversation.

"I went down to the springhouse this morning!" Taemestra let her shuttle fall and joined them.

"Against your father's orders." Nana shook her head and started twisting thread again.

Even Penelope was surprised. It wasn't like Taemestra to leave the house alone, especially on a sunny day like this one. Normally she would have taken Nana or Annyla and made them carry a parasol over her head so she wouldn't get sunburned.

"But how would I ever find out what's happening if I didn't go out?" She grabbed Nana's old hands. "Shouldn't Penelope and I be preparing for Father's return rather than spending our time in this dusty old room?"

Penelope wondered why Taemestra had waited until now to share such important news.

"I don't think it's your father you want to impress." Nana sighed. "Go on."

Taemestra ran from the room, then turned back at the doorway. "Can you fetch the water for my bath." It wasn't a question, but a demand.

Penelope glanced at Nana; she looked too old to carry the huge jars of water anymore.

"Yes, I'll bring them." Nana started after Taemestra, but paused when Annyla left the room.

"There are many stories about the shadowy night creatures," Nana whispered, as if she were afraid that Annyla or Taemestra might have lingered at the door. "But you must hear about the Followers from the moon priestess, not from your slave."

"You're my friend." Penelope felt close to Nana and didn't think of her as a slave.

Nana walked over to the loom and tore out the last threads that Taemestra had tangled, then lifted the threads forward and slid the shuttle, her eyebrows lowered in concentration. "You don't need more answers from me. Life will bring you more knowledge than you can bear."

She stopped, and her rough hand touched Penelope's arm, trying to give her comfort. She was about to say more when a deep bellowing voice came from the courtyard.

"Father!" Penelope bolted from the room and ran downstairs.

Her father walked across the courtyard, leaned his shield against a column, and took off his sword. He looked exhausted but happy, his nose sunburned and peeling. A deep slash, now scabbed and healing nicely, cut his arm. A purple bruise spread across his leg.

Penelope ran to him, then stopped and bowed her head to express her gratitude for his return. When she looked up, Taemestra was throwing herself into their father's arms. The girls pulled him inside and he sat on a stool with a padded seat. Annyla began removing his heavy sandals.

"I've come home from battle with surprising news," he said as Nana offered him a bowl of water and a smile.

"What?" Penelope asked. Her heart raced with excitement; maybe the men had made peace.

"Hector is coming to our home tonight with his father to negotiate a marriage." Their father smiled.

Penelope pressed her hand against her chest to steady her pounding heart. Could that be why Hector had looked at her so strangely? Did he want to marry her? She hadn't pledged her life to Selene yet. What would she do now? Against her will, her mind filled with images of Hector.

"I know he wants to marry me." Taemestra laughed happily.

"How do you know it's you he wants to marry?" Penelope asked, her chest empty, as if her heart had deserted her.

"I'll marry him in the winter month of Gamelion," Taemestra said easily, as if it were obvious Hector planned to ask for her. "We'll have a wonderful feast."

"He hasn't told me which daughter he's chosen for his bride." Their father tried to knit his eyebrows into a scowl, but a smile kept forming on his lips. "And I don't know if he can afford the dowry I'm going to demand."

"You pay the dowry!" Taemestra said.

"I do?" He shook his head. "Then I doubt I can afford to marry off either of my headstrong daughters."

Taemestra laughed again, her joy seeming to fill the air around her.

"I thought you liked Milon," Penelope blurted angrily. "You were flirting with him."

"Don't be foolish. Hector is the one I want." Taemestra stretched and brushed her fingers through her hair. "I even pointed him out to you, don't you remember? The soldier with the radiant dark hair?"

Penelope nodded. "I thought you were pointing to Milon."

"I only flirted with Milon and Eteocles to make Hector jealous, so he would want me more." Her dark eyes glittered with satisfaction.

"I'm happy for you." Penelope tried to smile, but her lips froze in an angry imitation of happiness. Jealousy and rage stomped through her.

She didn't understand Taemestra's duplicity; why would she flirt with one man when she wanted another? She sat down, no longer able to stand.

"Are you all right?" her father asked.

"Yes," she lied. Her stomach and chest felt as if they were filled with stones. "It's the heat of the day."

"I need to find Nana and ask her to start weaving the must luxurious cloth for my wedding day." Taemestra hurried off.

CHAPTER NINE

THAT NIGHT PENELOPE crept across the courtyard, breathing in the rich aroma of bay leaves and garlic drifting out of the kitchen. She tiptoed past the sleeping Nicias and opened the gate, the iron latch cold in her fingers. Loud laughter came from the *andron* and she hesitated for a moment, trying to pick out Hector's voice from the mix; then she stepped into the street.

A sudden gust caught her cloak and snapped it open like a sail. She snatched it back, wrapped it tightly around her, closed the gate, then bent her head against the wind and hurried down the walkway. She couldn't bear to stay in the house while her father negotiated Hector's marriage to Taemestra.

She had spent the afternoon trying to talk herself out of her feelings for Hector, but the more she thought about him the more her infatuation grew. The gods must have conspired against her. Maybe Eros had stunned her heart with an arrow and made her fall in love. Or perhaps Aphrodite had afflicted her with this terrible, sweet desire.

In the end she had decided to cherish her heartache. Aphrodite punished anyone who dishonored her by rejecting love, and Penelope already had too many problems without adding an irate goddess.

The moon was overhead when she rushed up the temple ramp, anxious to be indoors. Wind blasted against her, ripping at her tunic as if malevolent spirits were trying to bar her entrance. She slipped from her sandals and stepped through the columns to the windless air inside. She slowed, suddenly cautious, then froze. Something was wrong.

Flames crackled in the marble disk in front of the statue of Selene in her moon chariot, but no sound came from the vast hall. Usually soft footsteps and murmured prayers filled the *cella*. Now an eerie silence wrapped around her. Where could everyone have gone? If anyone were there, surely they would have come to greet her. She listened for the whisper of linen against the marble floor, and when she heard nothing, she cautiously stepped to the altar, the fiery eyes of the stone horses watching her with scorn.

Twisted gold and silver bands remained on the delicately carved surface where the gleaming moonstone had once shot out light. Penelope traced her fingers over the gold, wondering who had dared desecrate the temple the week before and steal the stone. The broken metal vibrated and writhed beneath her hand, sending waves of magic through her. Her skin turned beautifully luminescent. She jerked back, but the strange sensation still pulsed through her.

A distant sound made her look up. She was certain it had come from the inmost part of the shrine. She fixed her attention on the huge wooden doors, inlaid with silver crescent moons, behind the altar. She had never been allowed into the inner sanctuary, but maybe someone inside needed her help. Did she dare go where she had been forbidden to enter?

Even as she was considering what to do, her feet marched resolutely around the altar and statue toward the doors. She pressed her ear against the wood and listened for what might be on the other side. Her fingers found the heavy handle and inched the broad door open. She expected to be greeted by lurking shadows; instead sweet-smelling air hit her with sudden relief. She stepped in and let the door close behind her.

Moonlight poured through an opening in the roof, reflecting off a rectangle of water leading to a giant statue of Selene. Narcissus and roses made a path from the door to the water's edge. Their intoxicating fragrance was mixed with the smoky aroma of incense burning on pedestals on either side of an altar in front of the water. The bluish smoke twisted into the air, circling up to the heavens.

Penelope stepped forward, her feet crushing rose petals, and immediately felt the presence of someone behind her. She spun around, but she didn't see any movement in the shadows near the doors.

She turned back and again started toward the shimmering water. The only sound was the rustle of flowers beneath her bare feet. She had taken three steps when a noise startled her. She whipped around, eyes unwavering, searching. One of the immense doors to the sanctuary was slowly closing.

She gasped as cold fear rushed up her spine. She stepped back, rapidly scanning the shadows near the entrance, and stumbled into someone. Hands grasped her shoulders and she wrenched around, ready to fight the intruder.

Pandia stood behind her, a questioning look in her eyes.

Penelope's face burned with the blush working its way up her cheeks. "I know I'm not allowed in here." The words flew stupidly from her mouth. "But I didn't see anyone in the temple.

So I came in. . . . I thought . . ." She stopped. She was the most ridiculous person ever granted life. Surely now Pandia would take her amulet back.

But Pandia only smiled. "I've been waiting for you."

"You knew I was coming." Penelope twisted her fingers into her tunic so Pandia wouldn't see her nervousness.

"I sensed you were ready."

Penelope looked around. No one had come to witness her initiation, to dance or sing hymns celebrating her joy. "Where is everyone? Shouldn't a high priestess be here?"

"Your ceremony is different from all others," Pandia answered. "Your vow, more sacred."

"Mine?" Penelope felt suddenly dizzy. Why should hers be different?

Pandia took her hand and led her to the edge of the pool. The water lapped against her toes, warm and inviting.

"The hooded man you saw on the street with the soldier that night was the Atrox in its human disguise," Pandia explained.

Penelope felt a sudden chill, recalling the memory.

"You witnessed something most people see only as victims," Pandia continued. "The Atrox stole the young soldier's hopes and dreams."

"The mist that came from his mouth . . ."

"That was his spirit." Pandia nodded solemnly. "The Atrox stole it and fed it to the godless demons in its entourage."

"He's dead now?" Penelope rushed on, feeling guilty. "I didn't know how to save him." But even if she had known, she didn't think she would have had enough courage to do anything.

Pandia touched her arm as if she understood and was trying to comfort her. "The soldier is alive, but without his will. He'll remain a slave to the Atrox until he proves himself worthy of becoming a Follower."

"Does he become one of those shadow creatures, then?" Penelope shuddered. That seemed like a fate worse than death.

"The power to change shape and slide over the dark is a gift from the Atrox. The soldier won't receive that skill unless he pleases the Atrox in some way. Some Followers also receive an earthbound immortality that binds them to the Atrox for eternity."

Penelope's heart raced. She was standing on the edge of something important, and she wasn't sure she wanted to hear what Pandia would say next.

"The Atrox must be stopped," Pandia continued. "The number of its Followers is growing daily."

"What part am I to play in all of this?" Penelope asked, suddenly frightened of the answer.

"In human form the Atrox can seduce and deceive too easily," Pandia explained. "You must bind it to its shadow so it can't take human form again."

Penelope began to shiver. "But I have no power or magic. How can I fight it?"

"Let the future unfold and you'll find your way."

"Just wait for an idea to come to me?"

Penelope asked, baffled and upset. "That's not the way my father fight his battles. He studies and strategizes."

Pandia shrugged. "Maybe you'll do the same."

"You must have something more to tell me," Penelope said, her frustration growing.

Pandia held out her hand. "Do you still wish to dedicate your life to Selene, knowing now what your promise will be?"

"Yes." The word came out before Penelope had even had a chance to consider her answer. It echoed through the sanctuary with such force that Penelope felt certain she couldn't have been the one who spoke it.

"This has always been your destiny," Pandia explained. "The Atrox knows and will try to stop you. Making your vow will only increase your danger."

"I'm ready," Penelope answered with a determination she didn't feel. She bent her head, ready to receive Selene's blessing.

"Step into the water to purify yourself first," Pandia whispered.

Penelope slipped from her clothing, feeling no embarrassment, only wanting the luxury of the moonlight on her naked skin. She stepped into the pool. Water sputtered around her ankles, then her calves, pulling her deeper. For a moment she struggled against going under; then she dove. When she reached the bottom, she looked up through the rippling water, past the statue of Selene, to the night sky.

Moonlight overwhelmed her. The milky glow spun around her, becoming brighter and brighter. Her chest ached with its unbearable beauty, and at the same time something pure and longed for penetrated her being, flowing through her with pain and pleasure. She gasped at the strength of this newfound power and closed her eyes, but when she tried to open them again, another force kept them shut. Even with them closed, she could sense the terrible brightness of the moon's silver radiance.

For a while she lost consciousness underwater or thought she had passed out. When she came to, she was floating. She blinked and stared up.

The moon overhead seemed close enough to kiss. The air quivered with its magic. She had had a vision, and in it Selene had revealed sacred mysteries, but then the goddess had given her something to drink to make her forget.

Penelope was certain it had only been a dream, but the sweet taste of honey, mint, and barley meal remained in her mouth, and a lingering feeling of terror and anguish still filled her heart. What had Selene told her? She tried to recall, but the last hazy fragments broke apart and, like a dream, floated into unconsciousness.

A draft raced across her face and she remembered she was naked in a public sanctuary. She shot up, splashing water, and looked around, imagining a stunned throng of worshipers at the pool's edge, watching her. But the temple was dark, empty, and cold.

"Pandia!" Her voice echoed back so loudly she winced.

She stepped from the pool. Water ran down her back and streamed onto the marble floor. She picked up her tunic to dry herself and accidentally touched the amulet hanging from its chain. It burned the side of her hand as if it had absorbed some terrible, fiery power. She became aware of a searing pain on her chest and looked down. The ornament had scorched the image of the moon into her skin.

She leaned over the pool and cupped her hands, then splashed water on the charm. Steam rose. The talisman was cold now, but she could still feel the power of the moon running through it.

"Pandia." Where was she? Penelope had a thousand questions to ask her. Did this complete her ceremony?

She stood again and grabbed the edge of the altar as she suddenly remembered what she had promised to do. Dizziness and nausea overcame her. What audacity had made her think she could fight a force even the ancient gods had not defeated? She began to tremble. The gods always punished such pride.

She slipped into her wet tunic, wrapped her cloak around her, and ran to the doors. She leaned against one, pushing hard, then squeezed through the opening and shot past the statue of Selene in her chariot. At the entrance she bent over and fumbled with her sandals. Hot tears ran down her cheeks and fell to the temple floor.

At last she headed down the ramp. Wind blustered around her as wild as the emotions whirling inside her. She had almost reached the narrow pathway between the houses when a shadow moved. She leaned against the wall and wiped at her tear-blinded eyes, trying to clear her vision. Dark pressed around her, but she didn't see any apparitions lurking in the gloom.

She folded her arms over her chest against the cold and studied the darkness again. Maybe the movement had only been a trick of the wind-storm and her tear-blurred eyes. Or perhaps the ceremony had left her overwrought and filled with worries about the Atrox and its Followers.

She quickened her pace, shivering, anxious to be home, and headed down another tight corridor. Wind chased at her back, hurrying her along. She eased around a line of vases smelling of olive oil and stopped.

Someone stood in front of her. She couldn't see his face in the dark, only the outline of his body, looming above her.

Whoever it was stepped forward.

Fear seized her, but instead of turning to run, she stayed her ground, ready to fight.

CHAPTER TEN

PENELOPE SWUNG and hit hard muscle.

"Why are you striking me?" Hector grabbed her elbows, his laughter filling the night with sweet joy.

"Hector?" Her hand remained on his stomach, fingers spreading with a will of their own, sliding up his chest to his face.

"You frightened me." Other words raced to her mouth, but her mind cut them off. She couldn't confess her feelings to someone pledged to her sister. With rising embarrassment she realized her hands were still on him. What was she doing?

She quickly dropped her hands and started walking back the way she had come, not trusting her body to remain so close to his.

"Why are you running from me now?" he asked, hurrying along beside her. "I liked it better when you were staring at me as if I were a god."

"I wasn't." She increased her pace until her thigh muscles burned. "I was trying to see who was hiding in the shadows."

"But I saw you clearly." There was a lightness in his voice that surprised her. Had she only imagined it? He touched her hair. "Have you been bathing at this late hour?"

"Yes." She stopped suddenly, realizing that her damp tunic was clinging to every curve of her body. Her face flushed with embarrassment, and she wrapped her cloak more tightly around her.

She changed direction, heading for the cover of darkness within the grove of olive trees, and tripped over a fallen branch. Hector caught her before she fell and held her tightly. She leaned against him, savoring his warmth, stealing his embrace for a memory she could cherish forever.

At last she pulled away and edged into the shadows under a gnarled tree. "How did you know you'd find me here?" she asked, slowing down.

"Your slave Nana told me to go to the temple of Selene," he answered, keeping pace beside her.

"I guess you couldn't wait to tell me your good news." Her heart ached.

"I thought you'd be more excited," he said, obviously unaware of the pain he was causing her.

"I think you and Taemestra will be happy together." A sudden gust whipped around her, pilfering her words. She started to congratulate him again, but the puzzled look on his face made her stop.

"Taemestra?" He pulled her to him, his body protecting her from the wind.

"Yes." She struggled to keep her voice even.

"Is that why you think I'm here?" he asked.

She took a breath. "You came to tell me of my sister's marriage."

"Now I understand why Taemestra was so angry." He started walking again, deep in thought.

"Angry?" Penelope followed him. "What happened? Wouldn't my father give the dowry you asked for?"

"My father and I accepted what your father offered." He stopped under a tree, the leaves thrashing overhead.

When she stepped close to him, he clasped her hand and brought it, palm open, to his lips. Her heart skipped faster, and even though she knew it was wrong, she eased against him, letting herself feel his body. Then she thought of her sister and jerked away.

She imagined the gods laughing at her awkward, lovesick heart. She pulled away from him and dashed between the trees. Sticks and dried leaves crackled beneath her sandals. The wind chased after her. She was going to go back to the temple and spend the night there. She couldn't tolerate another moment with Hector, knowing he was promised to another.

"I didn't negotiate for Taemestra's hand," Hector yelled after her.

She stopped and whirled around.

He was suddenly beside her, his hands holding her face.

"I asked for permission to marry you, and even though I'm young to marry, both your father and mine have given their blessing."

"Hector," she whispered, overwhelmed by her feelings.

She looked into his eyes and a sweet danger awakened inside her. Eros must have shot another arrow into her heart, because desire raced through her, fierce and delicious.

CHAPTER ELEVEN

T HE NIGHT breeze blew through the trees overhead, soft with whispers and bringing the ocean damp with it. Hector caressed Penelope's back, pulling her to him as if he sensed the fire racing through her. He bent down to kiss her, but she turned her head before his lips touched hers.

"I can't marry you, Hector," she whispered.

His hands dropped to his sides, and even in the flickering shadows she could see the hurt in his eyes. "I thought you'd be happy," he said.

She let out a long sigh, searching for the right words.

"The marriage has already been negotiated," he said, his eyes suddenly angry.

"I want to marry you, but I can't," she started to explain, her voice shaky.

"Wait." He seemed to sense her turmoil. He removed his cloak, spread it on the ground in front of an uneven stone fence, clasped her hand, and helped her sit; then he took off his sword and scabbard and set them against a gnarled tree trunk.

She waited, sheltered from the wind, breathing the pungent sweetness of gray-green olives.

At last he sat down and wrapped his arm around her. "Now tell me why you think you can't marry me." He looked at her, his love unconcealed. "Whatever stands between us, I'll conquer. I promise. Nothing can stop us from being together, not even the deathless gods."

Penelope pressed her hand on his arm. "Don't say more," she whispered. The gods always punished such vanity.

"Tell me," Hector urged.

"I've dedicated my life to Selene," she began.

By the time she had finished, the wind had stopped, and a strange stillness had crept over the night.

Hector thought for a long time, then looked at her with hope. "Such a vow can be broken—"

"It's sacred," she argued. "I made a commitment to the goddess."

"Your promise has no meaning, because this evil god you're talking about doesn't exist. If it did, don't you think Athena would have sent the army against it before now? Such beliefs are superstition. Nana has told you too many stories."

"I've seen—"

He leaned over her, his eyes filled with desire. "Break your vow and marry me."

"I can't," she answered, her lips inches from his. "Even if I hadn't pledged my life to Selene, I still couldn't marry you."

"Why not?" he asked, surprised.

"My sister loves you," she answered.

"Taemestra?" He laughed. "She loves Milon and Eteocles. Maybe others, too."

"It's you," Penelope said flatly. "She flirted

with them only because she was trying to make you jealous, so you'd want her more."

"She'll find another, Penelope. And anyway, don't you want to know how I convinced my father to let me marry?"

She shrugged. The thought hadn't occurred to her.

"My father warned me that falling in love was a dangerous illness." Hector moved closer, his lips brushing against her cheek. "He didn't want me to marry, but I told him that when I saw you, my destiny opened in front of me."

"I felt the same." She closed her eyes, enjoying the closeness of his body.

Without warning he pulled away, his body tense, eyes alert and searching.

"What's wrong?" she asked, rising to her knees.

He didn't answer. Instead Hector quickly shifted his body. He crouched low, knees bent, the backs of his thighs resting on his calves, and reached back, fingers curling as if searching for the hilt of his sword; instead of finding the pommel, his hand closed on air. He turned and stared at the scabbard and belt resting against the tree trunk.

"What is it?" Penelope whispered, cold fear rushing through her.

Hector lifted his hand, cautioning her to be quiet; then, staying close to the ground, he crept to his weapon.

Penelope glanced around.

Tendrils of fog curled in from the ocean like fearful specters writhing around the trees. A curious chill prickled over her, seeping below the skin. Was that what Hector's battle-ready senses had picked up? The air felt tense, as if something were about to happen.

Hector drew his sword with a scrape of metal on leather and, still squatting, turned on the balls of his feet.

A billowing cloud stretched toward them, winding its way up the path. It looked like thick smoke, but the smell was wrong, rank and tainted with death. Soft chanting filled the night, and then a dim, orange glow penetrated the dark at the edge of the olive grove.

Hector stepped back, drawing her against him and half-dragging her behind a tree.

A man came through the roiling mists, walking toward the fence.

Hector bent low, body taut, ready to attack, his breath coming in long even draws.

Soon, others followed the first man, in single file, carrying torches, faces hidden beneath the folds of their cloaks, their monotone voices unnerving.

Penelope cringed. They were the same shadow creatures she had seen before. Were they searching for her again? Her heart raced.

Moonlight pierced the twisting black vapor, and the soldier came into view, trudging at the end, his eyes wide yet unseeing, his steps more sure now. He was dead, but by some magic alive.

"They're Followers of the Atrox," she whispered to Hector.

"Traitors, you mean." Hector stood and stepped after them, sword high. "They're going to the city wall. Probably to let the Spartan enemy inside."

She clutched his arm, fearing for him. "Don't go. They're too dangerous."

He jerked his arm free and frowned. "Do you think I'm a coward? I've never backed away from an enemy."

He tromped after the procession, marching to a certain death.

CHAPTER TWELVE

HECTOR WAS TOO close to the Followers, his boldness tempting fate. Soon one of them would hear his pounding footsteps and turn. Penelope ran after him.

"We have to hide," she begged him.

But Hector would not turn away.

"They're the ones I warned you about." She tugged at his arm. "You can't fight shadows."

"I see men, not shades." He shook her away and stepped forward, resolute.

"If they're traitors, then isn't it better to

follow in secret and see what they're planning? What good will it do to fight them?"

He hesitated, eyes watching the soldier disappear into the mist; then, with new resolve he took her hand and led her to a hedge of overgrown grapevines. They followed as close as they dared from behind gnarled branches and large flapping leaves to the city wall.

The procession filed into an underground passage dug near the stone base and hidden from the sentry walk.

"They're leaving the city." Hector paused. "Go back and tell your father I'm following them."

"I can't leave you." She was too afraid that if she did, she might never see him alive again.

"Then come with me." He crept to the gaping hole and started into the chamber.

Penelope followed him. A pale glow from distant torches lit the walls. The burning twigs filled the air with smoke and left a trail of black soot overhead. The chanting echoed inside the narrow space, magnified and vibrating through

Penelope. The eerie monotonous pitch chilled her.

They had gone a short distance when the light began to fade.

"We're lagging too far behind." Hector took her hand, increasing their pace.

They slipped around a craggy outcropping and bumped into the soldier trailing at the end of the procession.

Penelope sucked in air and froze. Her eyes darted to the Followers turning down another passageway.

The soldier looked at her with a dead stare, and his mouth dropped open as if to shout.

Hector thrust his sword at the man's throat, but before the blade struck, the soldier blinked, and his gaze became unfocused. He seemed to have forgotten what he had been about to do. His jaw snapped closed, and he wobbled, then turned in a sluggish way as if his muscles had become too heavy for his bones to carry. He started forward, his body shifting from side to side.

Hector stared after him, mystified. A sheen of sweat glistened on Hector's forehead.

Penelope released the air from her burning lungs. "We need to go slower," she cautioned.

But Hector lunged forward as if the peculiar encounter had intensified his curiosity.

She trudged after him.

When they came out of the cavern, they stood in a burned field, the smell of cinders and ash mixing with sea brine. Wind rustled against their ears, replacing the dreary chanting, and swept the mists away.

Penelope pointed toward the sea, sparkling with moonlight. "There."

A single torch fire bobbed, then disappeared.

"Hurry." Hector took her hand, his grip strong.

They ran to the edge of a cliff and studied the trail of torches on the rocks far below. One by one the torch lights vanished.

"They must be going into a cave." Hector scanned the rim of the sheer bluff, looking for a way down.

"Here." Penelope twisted the end of her tunic

into her hand and started on a narrow path cut between jagged boulders. She could feel Hector winding down the incline behind her, his sword scraping against the rocks. She concentrated on the moonlit trail, trying not to think of what waited for them.

Halfway down, the rocks became more slippery and her steps more careful. Waves crashed against the outcropping, and salt spray misted over her.

At last she came to the mouth of the cave and stared into the cold blackness; a stench of sulfur filled the air. She stepped back, heart pounding.

Hector pressed in front of her. "We've uncovered some plot to defeat Athens," he said, the excitement rising in his voice. "They must be meeting with Spartan leaders."

She shot him an angry look. "How can you forget the evil feel in the air back at the olive grove or the odd way the soldier behaved? Isn't that proof that what I told you is true? These aren't traitors. They're Followers of the Atrox."

He glanced at her, his doubt apparent, but he started forward anyway.

She dodged in front of him. "I think they're performing some rite, and the Atrox might even be inside with them."

He shoved past her, and plunged into the dark, his sword leading the way.

"Hector," she whispered, trying to call him back. Her frustration and anger made her break into tears. Where was her bravery? She had thought that after being initiated into the mysteries of the moon, she would be bold and courageous. Then she realized her fear wasn't for her own safety; it was for Hector's. She forged after him.

Crabs scuttled over her toes. She kicked them away, and her tunic caught on barnacles. She ripped it free and stumbled back. Her eyes shot up, fearful the sound might have carried down the cavern, but the drone of chanting was too loud.

She turned, staring back at the entrance. Cresting waves capped with foam rushed at her.

When the tide was high again, the cavern would be filled with water and hidden. Soon the sea would seal the entrance. She hurried forward, splashing through puddles, not wanting to be trapped inside with the Followers. She tried to show Hector the rising surf, but he seemed hypnotized by something in front of him. She followed his gaze.

Sparks scattered into the air like a flurry of red butterflies, twisting and landing on stones. The embers continued to burn, but the water trickling down the cavern walls didn't steam over the blazing cinders. Instead it froze into thin, glittering blue icicles.

Penelope shivered from the sudden chill, and her breath became white vapor. She crept forward and peered over a jutting rock.

Twenty men and women circled a huge fire. She should have felt its heat, but instead her fingers went numb with bitter cold. The inferno crackled and raged as if consuming a huge pile of wood and dry brush, but nothing fueled it. The flames hissed and flared from the black rocks on the grotto floor, and spectral frost spread out from the center in an ever-widening circle.

A girl stepped to the edge of the fire, her black hair iridescent. She traced her fingers through the flames as if she were intoxicated from the smoke and couldn't feel its burn. Then she dropped her tunic and stood naked before the blaze. Flames shot out and wrapped around her back like loving hands guiding her into the conflagration. She took one step forward and then another.

Penelope bit her lip to keep from screaming. Blood trickled into her mouth. She started to rush forward to save the girl from the obscene human sacrifice, but Hector grabbed her wrist and held her tight.

Fire seeped around the girl, sinuous and serpentine, stretching like tentacles into her hair and around her neck, gliding over her, leaving spiraling designs in its path. She lifted the flames and let them fall in a stream over her body as if she enjoyed the liquid feel of their caress.

Penelope had the oddest feeling that if she

could see the girl's face, her countenance would have been one of euphoria, not anguish. What was she witnessing?

Tension gathered in the air. The fire stirred with fury, sweeping higher, almost rising with excitement as the chanting reached a crescendo.

A darkening shape became distinct on the other side of the blaze. Shadows swept into it, thickening and growing until a tall man stepped from the dark and stood behind the veil of flames.

Hector took in a sharp breath.

The chanting stopped. Ominous silence followed, and the air filled with the presence of pure evil.

The man smiled at the girl and she threw back her head, shaking her long beautiful hair, and smoothed her hands down her body.

"Let's go." Penelope dug her face into Hector's shoulder, her teeth chattering. She couldn't bear to see more.

Hector nodded and, bending low, started back the way they had come.

Penelope crept after him, her sandals cracking the thin sheets of ice covering the puddles.

At the entrance waves raced toward them, the water thigh-deep now. Penelope struggled through the cold frothing surf, then stepped onto a rocky shelf and stumbled up the path, her heart racing with fear. She kept glancing back over her shoulder, terrified the Followers were chasing after her.

Finally she stood at the top of the bluff, wet and grateful to breathe the clear night air. She lifted her face to the moon and prayed to Selene.

"Any evidence of what we've witnessed will be washed back out to sea," Hector said, as if feeling the burden of trying to prove what they had seen. "What are they?"

"People who are dedicated to destroying the good in the world." She breathed through her mouth, trying to calm her jittery stomach.

"I'm sorry I didn't believe you." Hector seemed deep in thought as he sheathed his sword.

She looked over the edge of the cliff, wanting

to be back in the safety of her home. "I know."
She had an odd feeling that the ceremony would
end and the Atrox would become aware of them.
She shuddered, remembering the way it had used
some form of trance to draw her to it the night
Pandia had rescued her.

"Let's go," she said, and started walking.

She hurried across the burned-out field,
Hector at her side. Her feet stirred the scorched
earth into small puffs of dust. When she entered
the tunnel under the city wall, her wet tunic was
covered with black cinders. She held her hands in
front of her, feeling her way through the dark. By
the time she reached the other side, her fingers
and arms were cut and bruised. Hector had a
bruise over one eye.

"They can't be human." Hector looked at her
questioningly. "Are they immortal?"

"I've told you all I know," Penelope answered
with a sigh. "I wish I had the answers, but my
mentor seems to think everything I'll need to
know will come to me."

Hector nodded, but his eyes looked distant,

as if his mind were again trying to grasp what he had witnessed.

When they reached the front gate to her home a strange feeling came over her. "Let me stay with you tonight," she said, certain this would be their last chance to be together. "Please."

He shook his head even though his eyes were filled with longing. "I won't allow you to dishonor your father."

She started inside, the feeling of doom overwhelming her. She turned back and watched Hector walk away down the narrow street.

CHAPTER THIRTEEN

PENELOPE AWAKENED with a jolt. Sunlight stretched across her room in a golden haze. She wondered why everyone had let her sleep so late. Then she smelled the rich burst of onions and garlic cooking downstairs. If Nana was already starting dinner, then it was even later than she had first thought. She felt someone beside her and sat up, pulling a blanket around her.

Taemestra was balanced on the edge of her bed, obviously upset.

"What's wrong?" Penelope asked. Then she remembered the night before and felt foolish for her question.

"Wrong?" Taemestra clenched her jaw, her anger palpable. "Can't you guess?"

"I'm sorry." Penelope tried to take her hand, but Taemestra jerked back and frowned.

"I didn't mean for it to happen this way, but it did." Penelope climbed from bed and took the clean tunic she had laid on top of her chest the night before.

"So you're going to marry Hector?" Taemestra followed her. "What kind of magic did you use?"

"Magic?" Penelope stared at Taemestra in disbelief.

Taemestra rested a hand on her hip. "You stole Hector from me. I demand to know what charm or potion you used to bind a spell on him."

"I didn't." Penelope picked up the pin to fasten the cloth. Normally her sister would have helped her, but not today.

"Look at me." Taemestra stepped back and twirled around, weaving in and out of the sunshine in a sensuous dance. "Why would any man prefer you over me unless you used some magic?"

Penelope steadied herself. "You're only saying these things because your feelings are hurt. You'll find someone else."

"I don't want anyone else," Taemestra answered defiantly.

"We're sisters. We can't let a man come between us." Penelope reached out to embrace Taemestra, but she ducked away.

"Half sisters," Taemestra reminded her. "You think you've been so good to me, but you've never been there when I needed you. I had to rely on Nana, and she's no help at all."

"You don't mean that." Penelope touched Taemestra's hand, but Taemestra wrenched herself back, eyes on fire. Her hand flew up, and for one agonizing moment Penelope thought her sister was going to slap her.

Taemestra let her hand fall back to her side, but her loathing was clear.

"I can never marry Hector anyway," Penelope said, hoping to placate her sister. "I've already pledged my life to Selene."

"I don't want him now," Taemestra snapped. "And it's too late for you to try to appease me. I've made a commitment of my own."

"To another?" Penelope wondered if Milon had come by with his father and negotiated a marriage with Taemestra.

"Yes, another." Taemestra seemed calm now, but there was something odd in the way she looked at Penelope.

"Who?" Penelope asked.

Taemestra smiled contentedly. "I never did forget what happened that night at the festival a year ago. The men who chased us . . . I know what they are."

"Followers, you mean?" Penelope's heart raced.

Taemestra looked at her disdainfully. "Unlike you, I saw opportunity in what they offered."

"All this time you have lied to me?" Penelope

knew the answer, but her mind was spinning, unable to accept what her sister was saying. She clenched her teeth to stop her chin from quivering and blinked rapidly to hold back tears.

"They showed me what the Atrox offered. Do you really think I want to live as a woman must, cloistered away and spending my day weaving? That's one thing we have in common. We both want more. The Atrox offered me power and riches, every luxury I can imagine."

Penelope looked at her sister, remembering when they were younger. She thought of all the times she had helped Taemestra draw letters with her stylus on the waxed tablets and of the summer days spent with her picking flowers and watching the olive presses. The memories broke apart as a brutal thought came to her. "The ceremony last night."

Now it was Taemestra's turn to look surprised. "What ceremony?"

Penelope knew her sister well enough to know she was lying. She glanced down and saw the black soot rimming Taemestra's toenails. She shook her head, not wanting to believe, but knowing it was true. "You were the one who stepped into the fire."

Taemestra stared at her with cold hate. "How would you know about a fire?"

"I followed you last night." Penelope took a deep breath and tried to calm herself.

Taemestra focused on the small terra-cotta bathtub in which Penelope had bathed the night before. Her tunic lay crumpled beside it, stained black and ruined.

"So you followed me." Taemestra shrugged, and there was no shame or fear in her voice. "Then you should also know that you're the one who forced me to take such a path."

"Me?" Penelope asked, bewildered.

"The depth of my hatred for you made me do what I did," Taemestra answered through clenched teeth. "My need for revenge forced me to turn to the Atrox. It's your fault."

"It's not too late." Penelope tried to touch Taemestra, but she pulled away. "We can go to the temple of Selene and you can be cleansed."

"Why would I want that?" Taemestra asked. "Death no longer limits me."

"But you're a servant, a slave to—" Penelope's stomach knotted with grief.

"My master," Taemestra cut in. "The Atrox gave me immortality in exchange for Hector. It was an easy decision. If I can't have him, no one will."

"But why would it want Hector?" Penelope asked, stunned.

"I've sealed his fate." Taemestra couldn't stop smiling. She seemed to enjoy the misery she was causing Penelope.

"But if you love him—" Penelope stopped.

"You couldn't have loved him, but I do." Her words surprised her.

Taemestra's eyes flashed. "He's getting ready to leave."

"Leave?" Penelope didn't understand. "Are the men going to battle again?"

"While you were sleeping, I went to see him to congratulate him on his forthcoming marriage," Taemestra explained. "And he told me you couldn't marry because of the vow you had taken, so I told him that the only way to free you from your pledge was to destroy the Atrox."

"But why would you do that?" Penelope asked, her anxiety rising. "Aren't you supposed to protect it?"

Taemestra smirked. "Do you really believe Hector can defeat the Atrox?" She didn't wait for Penelope to answer. "I sent him to his death."

"I'll stop him," Penelope said with a confidence she didn't feel.

"There's nothing you can do." Taemestra leaned back on Penelope's bed, luxuriating in the moment. "He's getting ready now to go to Tartarus to find the Atrox."

"He won't go." Penelope stared at her sister, unable to believe the depth of Taemestra's hatred. Tartarus lay below Hades, a dreadful place where the wicked were condemned to live in eternity after death.

"His foolish love makes him blind to the consequences." Taemestra stretched her arms over her head. "No one has ever been able to go there and come back."

CHAPTER FOURTEEN

THE LATE AFTERNOON heat lay flat on the crowded agora, the air too hot and thick even for flies. Shoppers moved with slow steps past open stalls and slaves carried jugs of water on their shoulders at a languid pace, enjoying the cool drip of liquid down their spines.

Penelope hurtled through a group of men gathered at the shop of a shoemaker. They argued philosophy, trying to find truth. Their words brought a grim smile to her face. What would they do if they knew about the unbearable reality of the Atrox?

The men broke apart, faces startled by her disrespect, and gave her room to pass. She jostled around a bearded man at breakneck speed and accidentally stomped on his toe.

"Sorry," she said, swinging away from him.

"Penelope!" he yelled.

She glanced over her shoulder, but didn't stop running.

"I'm telling your father!" he shouted. "You're a menace. He'll punish you severely this time."

"That doesn't frighten me anymore," she said under her breath. She had much worse things to worry about.

She plunged sideways between two women carrying baskets, then shoved her way around a man stacking figs and pears.

After bursting past the last stall and the throng of people, she grabbed the hem of her tunic and yanked it up to free her legs. She sprinted through the olive grove, her reckless footfalls stirring dirt and dead leaves.

She had considered her options and finally decided she had only one. She had to break her vow and marry Hector to stop him from going on his deadly mission. She couldn't be responsible for his death. The thought made her eyes brim with tears. She bit her lip to fend off her need to cry. Everything had happened too quickly, and she couldn't think of anything else to do.

She ran up the ramp, heedless of the slow-moving worshipers, and dodged between them, almost colliding with a short woman carrying roses. She kicked off her shoes, her breath feverish, and wheeled inside, impatient to find Pandia. Sweat beaded on her forehead and gathered at the nape of her neck. She lifted her hair, but no breeze cooled her.

Frantic, she looked around. "Pandia!"

Worshipers looked up from their prayers and stared at her.

An old woman with gray braids draped over her shoulders stopped washing her hands in the stone basin. She pointed to a corner behind the statue of Selene.

Pandia stood alone, lighting incense at a small altar. Blue smoke writhed around her.

Penelope ran to her. Pandia looked up, but before she could say anything, Penelope threw herself into Pandia's arms. She leaned her head on Pandia's shoulder, needing the comfort of a mother.

Pandia embraced Penelope and caressed her hair. "What's wrong?"

Penelope wept.

"Have your trials begun so soon?" Pandia asked with sympathy in her voice.

"I need to be released from my vows," Penelope answered, her words breaking between sobs.

Pandia didn't try to argue her out of her decision. She didn't even seem surprised. She stepped back and placed a consoling hand against Penelope's cheek. "What happened?"

"It's the only way I can save Hector." Penelope sniffed back new tears. "My sister has tricked him into fighting the Atrox. He thinks he can destroy it and free me from my pledge."

Pandia nodded, her eyes soft and understanding. "You must be released, then. Immediately."

Penelope felt confused. Why was Pandia letting her go without even an argument?

"I—I'd hoped you'd know another way," Penelope stammered. "Some secret magic to stop him from going so I could keep my word to the goddess."

Pandia shook her head. "Whatever you decide. It's up to you."

"Are you sure there's nothing you can do?" Penelope felt bewildered. She had expected Pandia's scorn and ridicule, or at least an attempt to talk her out of her decision. She fell back against the wall, overcome. A distant memory stirred and she blinked. Someone was calling her name from a great distance, and then the feeling slipped away before she could dissect it.

"Few people can accept the burden that has been placed upon you," Pandia said gently.

"I'm sorry." Penelope bent her head in shame.

Pandia raised her hands, and as her fingers traced over Penelope's forehead, a cascade of silver sparks fell to the marble floor.

"You're released from your promise and free to marry Hector," Pandia whispered. "Let the future unfold as it was meant to be."

"Thank you." Penelope swallowed, her mouth dry, chest heavy with regret. She didn't understand why receiving what she had requested made her feel so terrible, but her emotions were too raw to allow her to consider that now. She slipped her hands under her hair to unclasp the amulet. "You'll need this back."

Pandia stopped her. "It belongs with you."

"But—"

"Hurry," Pandia cautioned. "Time is running out."

Penelope nodded and spun around.

"Remember Zeus in his wisdom gives us learning through suffering," Pandia called after her.

Penelope shrugged off the words. She had only one thought in mind. She dashed to the entrance, slipped into her sandals, and ran outside. Heat blasted around her. She held the hem of her tunic high, not caring who saw her shameless display. She needed to get to Hector's house before it was too late.

CHAPTER FIFTEEN

"HE'S LEFT ALREADY," Taemestra said, greeting Penelope as she reached Hector's home.

Nana stood behind her, sunburned and gripping a long pole that held a sunshade over Taemestra's head.

"Are you sure?" Penelope's chest tightened and her heart forgot to beat. The sweat on her forehead turned cold and she braced herself against the wooden door, imagining Hector lost in the shadowy underground kingdom. She turned to Nana. "Has he really gone?"

"I'm sorry." Nana glared at Taemestra, her hate unconcealed. "You couldn't have stopped him, Penelope. He had no will of his own."

Taemestra whirled around, knocking into the pole and making Nana stumble back. "If he had no will, it was because Penelope put a spell on him. I didn't need to do more than tell him where to go." She turned back, eyes smoldering. "It wasn't my magic that made him love so deeply."

"No," Nana said flatly, and adjusted the sunshade to cover Taemestra's face.

Soft weeping came from the other side of the gate.

"His mother's crying," Taemestra said without sympathy. "I imagine you don't feel much better, Penelope."

"I don't." Penelope breathed through her mouth, trying to stop the dizziness. She swallowed, but her throat caught. "Why did you make Hector believe he could defeat the Atrox? If you're so angry with me, why hurt him?"

"Because now you know how I felt when you stole him from me," Taemestra said with satisfaction. She started walking away, the hem of her tunic brushing over the dirt.

Nana followed her, squinting into the sun and holding the sunshade high for Taemestra. She glanced back at Penelope sadly.

Penelope leaned against the dusty wall, misery swirling inside her. Tears came painfully to her eyes and she couldn't hold them back, but even as she brushed the teardrops from her cheeks, she wouldn't allow herself to give in to her grief. She had to find another way to stop Hector.

That night Penelope wandered through the reeking slums of mud-brick huts pressed together along dark narrow alleyways. She carried cheese, olives, and bread wrapped in a piece of old linen, and a small jug of water. She paused, waiting for her eyes to adjust to the deeper darkness between two crumbling homes. The path was splattered with garbage and sewage.

Normally she wouldn't go this way, but her father wouldn't search for her here. He had restricted her to her room after hearing about her wild race through the agora. She would have been there still if Nana hadn't helped her escape.

The smell of salt air became stronger, and then the fetid odors fell behind her. She stood at the port, and a hundred burning torches lit her way. She breathed deeply and surveyed the small merchant vessels docked near the wharf. Timbers and ropes creaked and groaned with each roll of the sea. Larger ships anchored in the harbor basin.

She eased around sleeping slaves who worked as dockers during the day and searched for the man Nana had said would be waiting for her. She squeezed between stacks of cowhides and thick coiled ropes, then walked to the edge of the dock, her feet pounding hollowly on the wood planks.

"Here," a grating voice whispered.

She looked down at the shimmering water. A scrawny man stood in a small bobbing fishing boat. A huge eye was painted on the hull to ward off evil.

"Are you Er?" she asked.

"Who else would I be?" he said, his annoyance plain.

Clearly a slave, he wore a rough, homespun, wool cloth draped around his waist. Glaring white scars from whippings crossed his sunburned back, and he had been branded by many different owners.

"Do you want to go or not?" His piercing blue eyes stared back at her with contempt; obviously he didn't like the way she had studied him.

"I don't believe you have the right to take me away," she answered, fearful she might be accused of helping a runaway slave.

"And you don't have the right to go away without your father's permission," he snapped back.

She chewed on her lip. She had been foolish. "You've gone to Oceanus before?"

He nodded, but his eyes didn't meet hers. He looked up and down the pier. "If you want to go, get in. The night guardsman will be coming back soon."

Penelope wondered at his need for caution. The guard would be another slave hired out by his master to work the docks. They were probably friends. Instead of confronting him again she threw her bundle into the boat, handed him her jug of water, then climbed down a splintered ladder and stepped carefully onto the swaying deck.

"I'll take you only to the river," he cautioned. "No farther."

She nodded and stared back at the shore as they drifted away. Torch fires along the pier were reflected in the water, their golden rays stretching out across the bay. She wished she could have said good-bye to her father. With a shock, she wondered if this terrible sadness was how her mother had felt the day she went away.

Then she turned and faced the bow, staring at a black horizon. She was going after Hector. She couldn't live with herself if she didn't try to stop him. After that she had no plan. She didn't need one. She wouldn't be returning. No one ever had.

CHAPTER SIXTEEN

DAYS LATER IN her voyage, Penelope clasped the side of the boat and stared in wonder at the surging Oceanus. Surf rose high above her, blocking the sun, then dropped, water crashing over her and swamping the hull. The boat snapped and cracked, then rode up the next swell and down into the trough, only to crest again.

"There's where you want to go." Er grasped the tiller, his bony knuckles white, palms bleeding from his struggle with the currents to control the rudder.

Penelope got up on her knees, too afraid she'd fall overboard if she stood, her stomach queasy and trembling. She was certain the boat was going to capsize. Tempest winds slapped the small sail, and immense seagulls circled overhead, cawing and screeching.

A black line of beach stretched behind the frothing whitecaps, but seeing the distant shoreline didn't reduce her apprehension.

"All seas join here with the rivers of Hades," Er said. "The waters flow in and out two times in one day. Priests say the heavenly bodies descend into Oceanus at night and emerge from it during the day, but I don't believe it. Sunrise and sunset look the same here as on land. Maybe someday I'll go that far and see for myself."

"How often have you come here?" Penelope asked, breathing through her mouth to control her sick stomach. She didn't want to vomit again.

"Enough." His bloodshot eyes squinted at the skyline.

Penelope felt too ill to consider another journey here.

Er leaned against the tiller, and the boards in the hull creaked as the boat turned; then he threw a rusted anchor overboard. It did little to steady the boat.

"Only a fool wants to find Tartarus." His eyes darted to the shore as if he sought some danger worse than the raging water. "A man could fall for a year and not touch bottom there."

She stared at him. "You've been there?"

"Maybe." His leather face opened in a broad smile, revealing his toothless mouth. "You get off here. You'll have to swim to shore and find another vessel to carry you to Hades."

"How will I find another boat? I didn't see a fishing village."

Er laughed. "Don't worry. The waves are going to drown you before you even get to shore." He held out his hand for payment. "I got you here. That's all I promised, but I'll take you home for the same price."

"I'm staying," she answered with a confidence she didn't feel. She unwrapped the wet linen and picked out her mother's hairpins. The jewels flashed in the sun. She dropped three into his blistered and bloody palm.

He shook his head. "Only fools get off here."

She stood, sea foam spraying over her, and looked at the shore.

"Now!" he said with rising impatience and terror, as if he sensed the approach of something deadly.

She jumped and a wave hit her. She breathed in frothy water and gagged, then coughed and spit, trying to find air. The angry river thrashed around her. A wave broke on top of her and the current pulled her down. She kicked hard, clutching the linen in one arm and stroking with the other. Her lungs burned and bubbles escaped her nose.

She hit the surface with a huge gasp, then rolled over and desperately tried to swim, one hand splashing the water against the flow, but she made no forward progress. It was too late to turn back now; the boat with Er at the tiller was heading away.

Another wave collapsed on her, forcing her down. She tumbled in the current and lost her sense of direction. She opened her eyes and frantically searched the thick, churning waters for the surface, her lungs on fire. Her tunic billowed out, her hair twisted around her like a bed of sea kelp. Sand and broken shells roiled in the frenzied river, but she couldn't see which way was up. She tried to relax, hoping to float, but too afraid to swim for fear of diving the wrong way.

Her heartbeat thundered in her ears, then weakened. She began shaking violently from cold and wild fear, her chest and lungs wrenched with pain. Then she started to rise. She kicked and slammed through the surface with a gasp, her lungs exploding and sucking in air.

A swell battered against her. The rushing waters tossed her forward toward the rocky beach. She kicked, trying to hold back, afraid of smashing into the jagged boulders. Her toes brushed over something solid. She let out a startled cry, fearing that some carnivorous sea creature had found her; then her foot hit solid ground.

She walked to shore, legs wobbly and weak, and fell down on dry sand, her soggy knapsack clutched in her hands. She whispered a prayer between sputtering coughs, then fell asleep, her mind filled with gratitude.

When she awoke, the sun was high overhead. Trees stunted and wind-sculpted into ghostly shapes lined the shore. Their spare narrow leaves gave no escape from the dazzling white light. She stood and started walking, back aching, wind flapping her wet tunic awkwardly around her legs.

Broken vessels lined the rock-covered shore, their sails shredded. Frayed remnants snapped around their masts. She wondered how many sailors had tried to navigate the river and lost their way.

She climbed over boulders encrusted with barnacles as large as her hand and stopped in front of one small craft that looked as if it might still be seaworthy. She ran her hand over the weathered transom, then looked out at the river, searching the choppy whitecaps for a channel of calm water.

The savage, unrestrained power of the river made her lose heart; even if the boat did float, how would she navigate it? And if she actually managed to reach the mouth of Hades, she had no libations to pour for the dead, and without even a ram to slaughter for the gods, how could she expect success?

Her stomach pinched with hunger. She unwrapped the soggy linen, tore off a bite of mushy flatbread and drenched cheese, and started to put it into her mouth, then stopped and threw her food, shred by shred, to the sky, offering the gods all that she had.

Wind gusted down on her, and a storm of seagulls swept over her, cawing and catching the food in the air. The birds circled her, shrieking for more.

She hoped the gods were pleased with her sacrifice. She pushed the small boat into the water. The curved prow danced over the waves. She waited anxiously, but it seemed as if it would float. The sail was useless, the tattered shreds lashing around the weather-beaten mast. Broken oars lay in the galley. Maybe desperate sailors had used them once, trying to turn the boat back from the waters of Oceanus. Then another thought occurred to her. What had happened to their bones? She should have come across at least one skeleton. She stared at the hungry waves, sensing the sailors' fate, then pulled herself into the boat.

Tempestuous winds gathered behind her, blasting at her back, and even without a sail the vessel bobbed forward in a steady direction toward the west.

The waters turned gray-green, then black. Lightning flashed, and the boards screeched and rasped. Unrelenting waves broke over the prow, smashing down on her. The sky grew as dark as the sea, and the next lightning strike revealed the silvery mouth of a cave in an island directly ahead.

As she approached the opening in the crag, the rumble of cascading waters became louder than the screaming wind. Her heart lurched, and she grabbed the sides of the boat, her fingers digging painfully into the splintered wood. She had no way to turn the boat back. The noise became unbearable. Her stomach knotted as the bow tipped forward. She looked over the edge, down a seemingly bottomless pit. The boat plunged over a giant waterfall. Air slapped her face, the water's roar deafening. She clenched her eyes shut and clung to the bow.

The boat hit bottom with a terrible bounce, sending pain up her spine. The wood creaked and popped as the craft continued to skid over the water. Each bounce sent another agonizing shock through her.

Finally the small vessel settled and headed deeper into a subterranean passage, as if something were pulling it forward. She brushed her wet hair away from her face and frantically looked around, breathing in the sulfurous stench of decay. Cavern walls rose high above her in jagged peaks. The river, heavy with swirling mud, lapped at the boat with thick lazy sounds.

In the distance dogs barked, and her breath stopped; fear and wonder seized her. The howls came from Cerberus, the three-headed dog that guarded the entrance to the underworld, ensuring that those who entered never left. She stared into the misty air, trying to see the monstrous watch-dog, and at the same time shuddered, knowing it devoured anyone who tried to leave.

A dim greenish light lit a vast underground beach crowded with the transparent forms of the dead waiting to cross the miry river to the other shore. An old man with fire burning in his eyes slowly poled a boat.

"Charon," she whispered, awestruck.

She floated past the aged ferryman, who carried the dead in his boat across the river Styx to their final resting place in Hades, and felt an increasing sense of doom. She was breaking the law of the gods in navigating this river and entering the land of shades and night.

Something touched the back of her neck like a whisper. Rustling noises surrounded her. She spun around, cringing. Breath left her in a sudden scream. Spirits of the recent dead gathered in the air around her, thirsting to drink blood. They circled her, eyes

◄ 155 ►

yearning for life. If one touched her again, she thought, she'd start screaming and never stop.

Her boat hit the shore with a jolt, and she tumbled forward. She had crossed the river over which no soul returned. Her stomach clenched and she took deep breaths, trying to steel her courage. Her journey had just begun. Now she had to find Hector.

She forced her body to stand and step off the boat. Her foot slipped on the slimy bank. She let out a startled gasp, balanced herself, and sloshed through the ankle-deep water. The murky mud whirled around her, clinging to her feet and dragging her away from the shore. She grasped reeds on the water's edge and pulled against the current, then strained and ripped free, dragging herself onto the embankment.

She had barely caught her breath when a scream filled the cavern. Her heart thudded. "Hector!"

She ran up the slope toward the yell.

Gasping, she reached the edge of a precipice and glanced down.

Hector drew his sword and screamed a throat-splitting battle cry, then charged at a churning black cloud, his bronze breastplate and helmet reflecting fiery lights from inside the foul rolling vapor.

"Don't!" she yelled, and started down the treacherous path cut into the side of the gorge.

Hector thrust his sword into the immense swirling cloud. What had he seen in its center to make him think he could fight a mist?

He ran back and grabbed an arrow from his quiver and fit it in his bow. He pulled back the string and fired the shaft into the cloud.

A terrible shriek filled the air. Penelope clamped her hands over her ears, trying to block the barbaric wailing.

Hector stepped back, picked up his sword, and held it high, ready to strike, but the shadow cloud retreated, then the darkness gathered tighter, forming itself into a tall man. The Atrox materialized and stepped forward, an arrow through its side. Bending one knee, it offered Hector a gift of gold ankle bands. "In tribute," it said. "For defeating me."

"It's a trick!" Penelope yelled, trying to stop him.

But Hector had already clasped them around his ankles. He glowed with an odd internal light and then flames burst from him.

"Hector!" She ran to him.

He looked up, for the first time seeing her. His eyes met hers from behind the flames, full of pain and love.

She had failed him.

"I'm sorry," she mouthed.

Then he was gone.

She dropped to her knees and collapsed on the edge of the path, rage and grief stirring inside her; then, through her sobbing, she became aware of a change in the air. The hypnotic power of the Atrox fixed on her. The dark roiling cloud shot up the steep precipice, screaming toward her. She jumped and ran, blind with tears, over the narrow trail, her soggy tunic twisting around her legs. At the top of the summit she slipped and fell on her stomach in the oozing mud.

Black shadows writhed around her with the

sensuous slowness of a snake, binding her. Her skin crawled with the feel of the evil tracing over her. She squirmed away, stood, and raced over the slick slimy mud toward the river. She came to a yawning abyss, but instead of turning back she slid over the embankment and down the chasm, silt and wet warm earth gathering around her. She coasted down, the river rushing toward her, but when she glanced back, alarm surged through her. The shadow spiraled behind her, faster and faster. Its cold evil brushed against her shoulder as she plunged into the murky water of the river Styx.

The sluggish current rolled around her, dragging her out into the middle of the listless stream. The souls of the dead drank there, to forget their lives on earth, and that was all she wanted now. A sweet lethargy seeped over her, as if the murky waters were lulling her to sleep. She closed her eyes, longing for nothing more than to drift into dull oblivion. A welcome drowsiness replaced her terror. Her heartbeat slowed. She forgot to breathe. She could no longer remember what had frightened her. Souls of the dead fluttered around her in welcome. She floated on her back, staring at the vaulted cavern overhead, trying to recall life, but it was no more than a distant memory.

Splashing broke the silence. Ripples filled the waters, quivering to her in ever-widening circles. She glanced to the side, her eyes drowsy. A tall man with fiery eyes waded into the languid river. An odd halo of black shadow writhed around him.

She closed her eyes, the rhythm of his slow steps in the oozing stream seeming like a sweet lullaby.

His hands wrapped around her waist and he lifted her from the sleepy waters. She cried, wanting to return to the river, but he carried her to shore. The light was too bright, the sounds too many. Someone was whimpering and the cries annoyed her, until with a start she realized the pathetic moans were coming from her own chest. She blinked, trying to throw off her confusion.

Without warning, the arms holding her dropped her in the sand. White light blinded her, and the nearby surf crashed to shore. From the corner of her eye she could see the Atrox in human form. He stood over her, casting a long shadow across the beach.

She shook her head against the drowsiness and glanced up again. The sun shone brightly in her face. She sucked in air as memories slammed back to her, filling her with thoughts of Hector, the Atrox, Pandia, and Taemestra.

The Atrox grinned at her as if it had won, but she reasoned that if the sun was shining, then the roaring waves came from Oceanus and she was outside the Atrox's Tartarian domain. Er had said the waters flowed in and out of Oceanus two times in one day. Maybe she had drifted longer than she had thought and the stronger power of the river Styx had saved her from the hypnotic force of the Atrox.

She concentrated, gathering all her energy, then jumped up and slammed past the Atrox, shrieking a battle cry. She ran down the craggy shore, rocks cutting painfully into her feet.

Startled seagulls took flight, sweeping

around her, making it impossible for the Atrox, now an ominous shadow, to catch her.

She burst into the water and handed her life to Fate. The ancient sea goddess Tethys took pity on her. A giant wave crashed around her, submerging her in the savage surf. Cold spread through her, but instead of fighting it, she welcomed the numbness, knowing that the goddess had saved her from the Atrox.

CHAPTER SEVENTEEN

M

ANY NIGHTS LATER, Penelope be-
came aware of soft lapping surf tickling at her
toes. Her fingers curled into wet sand. She lifted
her head, feeling desperately thirsty. The scent of
smoking fish made her stomach tighten with
hunger. She coughed and licked her stinging, sun-
blistered lips. She was back within the city walls
of Athens. The tide was out and she lay on the
strand near the wharf. She offered a prayer of
thanks to the old Titan goddess and got up on her

knees. She tried to stand but fell back on the gritty shore, too weak.

Penelope blinked, her eyes burning, and stood again. This time she stayed, but her legs were stiff and unable to move. She rubbed at her sunburned thighs, then rearranged her tunic and took one faltering step after another.

The roll and clomp of donkey carts came from the pier.

After slowly making her way to the dock, she stole a ride on the back of a cart loaded with onions and leaned back, staring at the night sky. If anyone saw her riding by, they would have thougt she was a slave going home for the night.

Near her house, Penelope jumped from the cart and stumbled, then stood and walked to the gate. Her stiff fingers worked the latch, and then she shuffled across the courtyard.

Nicias snored loudly, a blanket gathered around his chin. She stole into the kitchen and greedily drank water from a jug. Her stomach felt cramped, and then she sipped more slowly. After stripping off her tunic, Penelope used the drinking water to wash the sand from her hair and face, not caring who might see her naked body. She stuffed her ruined tunic in the stove fire. Flames hissed and sizzled, finally burning the tattered cloth.

Making her way upstairs to her room, she closed the door behind her and fell upon the bed. She woke several times during the day and lifted her head only to assure herself that the shadows in her room were natural. Several times she was aware of her father sitting by her side and holding her hand. Nana fed her broth and gave her sweet wine to drink.

Late the next night, thirst awakened her again. She dressed in a crisp tunic and stepped down the stairs, the boards creaking familiarly under her bare feet. She had started for the kitchen when the front gate opened slowly as if someone were trying hard not to be heard.

Instinct told her to hide. She slipped back into darkness and watched from behind the stairs.

Three shadowy forms entered the courtyard. Then Taemestra stepped into the moonlight, her eyes flashing yellow like a cat's. Two men followed her around the altar to the reception room, their sandals scuffing against the pebbled floor.

"We have to stop the Magna Mater." A man spoke in a hushed voice.

Penelope wondered what the Magna Mater was.

"Who escapes Hades?" Taemestra whispered angrily.

"Your sister does," the other said.

Penelope froze, skin prickling. They were searching for her. Panic seized her as she realized she could have been asleep upstairs and unaware of their arrival.

"She is here." Taemestra started toward the stairs. "We'll have her now."

Footsteps came toward Penelope. She whipped around, frantically looking for another place to hide, then slid along the wall to the kitchen.

"I'm hungry," one of the men complained.

"Can't you wait until later?" Taemestra asked.

"Do you really think she'll get away?" he answered.

Taemestra snickered, and the sound of her insolent laughter sent a chill through Penelope. Her chest ached. She had lost not only Hector, but also her sister.

Penelope stood, hidden in shadow and holding her breath as they turned and walked toward her. She couldn't move now without being seen. They crossed in front of her, close enough to touch, and went inside the kitchen. Soon the smells of cheese and olives filled the air.

When she was certain they were busy eating, she stole across the courtyard, breezing through the moonlight into shadow. She paused at the gate and opened it with tender slowness; then she hurried out on the street and started toward the temple.

She had gone only a little way when she felt someone behind her. She spun around. She didn't see any movement in the shadows, but the feeling of being followed didn't go away.

"Who's there?" she called.

When no one answered, she touched the amulet still hanging around her neck and a sly smile crept across her face. She was tired of being prey. If the Atrox came for her again, she'd be ready. She glanced down at the stone. Words came to her, seeming on fire and ready to be said. What did she have to lose? Reciting the words would consume her, but what would happen to the Atrox? Would it be destroyed as well?

Then another idea came to her. Maybe her sister and the two men were stalking her. Did they want a challenge? She was ready.

She moved stealthily into the nearby shadows, the talisman vibrating in her hand, its power straining to be freed. She no longer feared death. Her heart took on the fast, sure rhythm of the predator. She crouched, feeling warriorlike, ready to spring.

A rustling sound broke the silence.

She listened. Maybe the wind had blown leaves across the dirt, but caution told her that Followers were surrounding her. She slipped into the blackness of a potter's shop, the dank clay smell wafting around her, and waited, nerves tingling, ready to pounce.

Furtive footsteps crept toward her, followed by an odd scratching sound on the dirt bricks. Then long fingers with curling yellowed nails slid into the moonlight brushing across the wall. A woman appeared, her thick, matted hair covering her eyes, her tattered and soiled tunic fraying where the hem dragged along the ground.

"Penelope," she called. "Don't fear me, my child. We need to talk."

CHAPTER EIGHTEEN

THE WOMAN SHUFFLED toward Penelope, her hand leading, tracing her sightless way along the side of a house.

"I have news of Hector," she said in a throaty voice, her wool tunic dragging behind her with the sound of snakes slithering across sand.

"He's dead." It was the first time Penelope had said the words, and new sadness settled on her, as heavy as a slab of stone.

The unkempt woman stepped into full

moonlight, and Penelope recognized her immediately. She was the blind seer who sat at the gate of the acropolis near the tiny temple to victory. People went to her with their private worries and questions.

"Take me to the temple of Athena and we'll see if he's dead." She stopped moving and stretched out her hand, searching for Penelope.

"Are you saying he's alive?" Penelope's heart raced. "He can't be. I saw the flames consume him."

When the seer didn't answer, Penelope clasped the dirt-caked hand and placed it on her own shoulder to guide the woman. They trudged through the narrow streets in silence, the seer's fingers digging into Penelope's skin; then they stepped slowly up the slope to the acropolis.

"Here." The seer stopped on the east side of the Parthenon.

Penelope turned.

Wind brushed the woman's thick matted hair from her eyes. Her milky white pupils shone with the moon's radiance. She cocked her head as if she heard a music that only the blind could hear and pointed to the night sky. "Your Hector wanders the universe alone."

"I saw him die," Penelope whispered.

The seer shook her head. "He was cast from earth and remains unable to return unless summoned by his master, the Atrox."

"How do you know about the Atrox?" Penelope asked, suddenly fearful.

The woman pointed to the tattoo on her neck. "I come from a Scythian tribe, north of the Black Sea, and was brought here a slave, then spurned when I lost my sight; but I gained a deeper vision."

"Tell me about Hector." Penelope wanted to believe he was still alive.

With the skill of the sighted, the seer gently wrapped her fingers around Penelope's head and turned her face to the heavens. "There he is, in the stars."

Penelope stared at the unfathomable depths of the universe, looking for a new constellation. "I don't see anything unusual."

"Do you see one star falling?" the seer asked.

"I see a shooting star," Penelope answered.

"This one will be different from any you have seen before," the seer assured her.

Penelope watched, expecting the light to flame out as the star approached the earth, but suddenly it changed direction. She squinted to make sure.

"That's your beloved Hector." The seer reached her crooked fingers out and marked the air as if she were inscribing it with some Scythian symbol to protect them from the Atrox.

Penelope's heart raced. Could it really be Hector? Her emotions vacillated wildly between despair and hope.

"Let me show you and remove all doubt." The seer took Penelope's hand, and when she touched her, Penelope became filled with Hector's emotions, his desolation and loneliness, anguish and love for her.

"The time you've been separated has been hard for you but immeasurably worse for him," she went on.

Penelope watched the shooting star, her heart aching. She let her tears fall.

"He can look down and see you as if there were no distance between you," the seer continued. "The Atrox allows him to watch you, because it knows that to do so causes him great pain."

"There must be a way I can free him," Penelope whispered.

"Yes," the seer said. "You must either join the congregation of the Atrox or destroy it."

"How?" Penelope asked. "How can I destroy something so powerful?"

"It's your destiny." The seer turned, ending the conversation, and then, stretching her hands in front of her and dragging her feet, disappeared into the shadows.

Penelope wiped at her tears and looked at the moon. "Please," she prayed. "Let me live to see the Atrox destroyed. I promise to forgo the peace of death until that day."

She closed her eyes in concentration, and when she opened them again, long writhing silhouettes flew across the moon. She looked out beyond the city wall, assuming the Spartans had set new fires, but the shadows she saw didn't come from smoke.

The sinuous figures turned and like flying snakes dove toward her. Was this what her prayer had conjured?

She sensed someone behind her and whipped around.

Taemestra walked toward her, carrying a small fire in her bare hands. "The Atrox heard your prayer and has granted your wish."

"I didn't pray to the Atrox." Penelope stepped back, apprehensive.

Taemestra heaved the fire. It sputtered through the air, throwing off a trail of sparks.

Penelope turned to run, but the shadows she had seen floating over the moon were suddenly behind her, spinning into tight coils. The black serpent forms curled around her wrists and held her as the dark vapors continued to bend themselves into the two men she had seen earlier in her house.

The fire hit her chest, but instead of burning, it circled her with penetrating cold.

"The flames burn away mortality and give eternal life." Taemestra smiled triumphantly.

"But at what price?" Penelope struggled, trying to escape the men holding her.

Without warning the small fire erupted into an inferno, its winds screaming around her. Flames danced and shot to the sky. Her fingers ached, cheeks stinging from the piercing cold. Blue frost traced a delicate pattern over her skin, ancient symbols of demons and evil.

Penelope cried out.

"Soon we'll be sisters again," Taemestra said, her eyes smoldering and reflecting the flames.

The men dropped their hold on Penelope and stepped back.

Penelope shuddered and swirled around. Something dangerous lurked in the raging fire. Then a black shadow wrapped around her. The foggy shape of a man stood beside her, its eyes wicked black points, its strong arrogant face challenging her.

"So you're the one sent to stop me." It spoke with a proud voice and stroked her shoulder.

She winced and pulled away, disgust rushing through her, but even as she hated its touch, it also awakened a forbidden hunger, and a pleasant thrill traveled up her spine.

The Atrox smiled as if it knew her secret thoughts. Too late she realized she had let down her guard. It was in her mind, sensing her revulsion and desire. Its grin filled with hideous confidence.

Fervent flames shot up in celebration, howling with desire, the swirling vortex slapping around her. Her heart throbbed, its beat slowing. The cold became unendurable and she began to cry, tears freezing on her cheeks. When she could bear it no more, the pain changed and burst through her veins with a sweet ache, filling her with deliciously evil and dangerous longings. She saw new possibilities. Why not give in and join the Atrox? Why continue the struggle?

The conflagration hissed louder, her flesh needing its touch. Shadow hands fondled her back, the caress intolerably arousing. She surrendered and stretched out her arms. But as she ran her hands over her body, her fingers touched the talisman, and the trance broke. She recoiled and tried to step away from the fire. The blaze grabbed her and drew her back, its soft swelling roar trying to comfort her.

In desperation she reached for the talisman, but the Atrox knew what she was trying to do; it pulsed into her head with unbelievable power. Her mind went blank and she couldn't quite remember why she had clutched the moon charm in her hand. An immense force told her to throw it into the flames.

Her fingers started to rip it from her neck, but then she caught herself. She drew in a chilling breath and struggled against the numbing force. With all her remaining strength she turned her eyes to the talisman and focused on the first word etched in the stone.

"Dingirmah." Power exploded inside her.

The Atrox looked at her; his hypnotic eyes flashed ice-blue. "You'll suffer for this." His lips twisted, then dissolved as he whipped away with the fury of raging winds.

Penelope tried to step away from the fire, but

it lashed around her, holding her tight. She held the talisman. She didn't understand the words or know what they meant, but somehow she thought they summoned the good in the universe, a power too strong to perceive. She took a deep breath and read the second word. *"Nimena."*

Flames sputtered and died. Icy sparks twisted into the air before cascading to the ground and melting.

Penelope wrapped her arms around her body against the gripping cold; her teeth chattered, and the force of the second word still flared inside her with frightening power. What would have happened if she had read the entire incantation?

"Your magic may have kept you from becoming a Follower, but it didn't stop the flames from burning away your mortality," Taemestra said with a contemptuous smile. "You'll always be connected to the Atrox now."

Still shaking, Penelope brushed away the frosty patterns covering her arms and face. "I'll destroy it," she promised with a surge of anger.

"If you do," Taemestra snapped back, "you'll destroy part of yourself as well."

Penelope knew that was true. She could feel the Atrox pulsing through her, but there was something else. A stronger power.

Taemestra smiled at Penelope's silence. "Don't you even wonder why the Atrox was so anxious to give you immortality when you plan to destroy it?" She didn't wait for an answer. "You failed to ask for perpetual youth. In granting your wish the Atrox has condemned you to age forever unless you join it."

Taemestra fell back into the arms of the man standing behind her; their bodies wove into the dark and then they reeled away, one shadow streaming through the night.

Penelope glanced at the moon. "I promise," she repeated.

CHAPTER NINETEEN

P ENELOPE SAT ON her bed, staring out the window at black clouds gathering in the western sky. Winds battered her shutters against the outside wall and skated into her room. Her father was downstairs, eating breakfast alone. She pinched her blankets, pulling them around her as if woven wool could protect her. She wished he'd come talk to her. She needed his advice.

A desperate sadness hung over her and seemed to make the air too thick to breathe. She had bathed twice, but water did nothing to remove the unclean feeling. Her body felt invaded, her life transformed into something unimaginable. She had no tears left to cry.

Distant thunder growled, and like a flicker of thought the Atrox was in her head again. A chill brushed over her skin, and she grimaced at the rich flavor of wine flooding her mouth. She spit and gagged but couldn't spew out the taste.

The Atrox laughed at her feeble attempt. *Our connection is too strong now,* its voice said, breezing across her mind. *You'll taste what I eat, smell what I breathe, touch whatever I kill, hear the screams I hear, until you decide to become mine.*

She grasped her amulet, searching for comfort, but the stone lay cold and dead in her sweating palm, the incantation gone. The letters etched in the surface had vanished, refusing to reveal themselves to her. Maybe she had wasted her one chance by not reading all the words the night before, or perhaps the charm felt the evil gaining power inside her and knew her predicament was hopeless.

You're no longer meant to have the talisman, the Atrox

whispered, taunting her. *Soon, someone who can see the words will take it from you.*

"Let me rest," she pleaded out loud.

But in answer her temples throbbed and the pain inside her head became unbearable. Her vision blurred, and then she was spirited away, kidnapped again. Her body remained in her room, wrapped in too many covers for the sultry day, but she was with the Atrox, roiling through billowing black vapor.

I can offer you everything. Its voice was compelling, and against her will she listened. *Join me and you can live in a palace greater than those on Olympus.*

"Never." She tried to fight it with mental force, but it seemed to enjoy her defiance and struggle.

You'll be mine soon, it promised with ruthless delight, and then it dropped her.

She fell back into her body, her head pulsing with the Atrox's evil. She blinked and found herself in her room again, but this time, when she opened her eyes, a savage smile crossed her face.

"Soon you'll be mine," she threatened back.

While her mind was in its captivity this time, a thought had slowly formed: if the Atrox could come to her at will, then she could also go to it. Everything felt perfectly clear now. Her skin prickled, but not from fear this time. Excitement rushed through her. It was a dangerous gamble, but it was her only chance. She had to find the telepathic link between them. If she could spy on it and find out where it dwelled, then she could go to it, catch it unawares, and destroy it.

She waited patiently now, and when it came again, she didn't resist.

You're weakening, it taunted her. *Or perhaps you're starting to see that you have no options.*

She hated the sinuous feel of it weaving inside her mind, but she let herself go, not struggling as it streaked through her, dragging her spirit away. At first she explored it hesitantly, searching for the bond between them, certain there must be a connection she could use. Careful with her thoughts, she seeped through its vast void, sinking into it, searching for the psychic tie.

To her surprise, the Atrox didn't try to stop her but seemed eager for her to know it. It drew her deeper into its stark cold nothingness.

When her fear became too great, she concentrated and pulled back. She returned successfully to her body. She blinked, looking around her room, then closed her eyes, opened her mind, and joined the Atrox again, feeling braver now that she had the ability to return.

Abruptly she became aware that she had found the connection. Not only had she found it, she had used it. Her heart raced, exultant, her thoughts reckless with jubilation. Could she follow the path again? She was certain she could. It was as simple as spinning thread from a bundle of raw wool. She tried desperately to calm herself, terrified the Atrox could sense her treacherous thoughts. She knew how to unite with it now.

But the Atrox mistook her excitement for eagerness. *Soon*, it promised. *Soon you'll belong to me.*

With a jolt it shoved her back into her body. When she was certain it had left her mind, she closed her eyes and followed after it down the telepathic link. Her head felt strange at first, as if she were falling into a deep trance. And just when she thought she wasn't going to be able to make the connection, she slipped away, leaving her body on the bed. She fell into an immense void, and then the emptiness opened, and in her mind she was traveling at an incredible speed through swarming shadows.

Without warning, she burst into light, wind snapped at her face, and the achingly beautiful countryside lay far below her, the smell of damp earth surging around her. She had successfully stolen inside the Atrox's being and was looking through its vision as it sped back to its home. The thrill of victory buzzed through her, and she delighted in all that she saw around her, savoring her vast view of the world.

The Atrox dove through clouds, flying like a bird, its speed unimaginable. Dazzling shafts of lightning lit the dark thunderheads, and rain came at her in sheets. Awestruck, she forgot to hide her presence.

Suddenly her bond with the Atrox tightened. She cringed and tried to pull back.

You followed me, it said with surprise.

She had expected its wrath but experienced its evil joy instead. She concentrated on the beauty in the lightning strikes, trying to hide her real reason for being with it.

I can give you more than this, it offered, sensing her awe. *Stay with me forever.*

The Atrox opened a whirlpool, sucking her down. Turbulent winds whistled around her. She tried to wrench herself free and return to her body, but the Atrox was too strong. She spiraled downward, certain it had known all along what she was planning and had set a trap of its own. Now she would be lost forever in its appalling memories. Disgust and revulsion made her stomach quiver. She plunged deeper, cold draining her warmth, her screams echoing around her.

Something wet splattered her forehead. At first she thought it was blood, but then thunder cracked across the sky, the crash vibrating through her. She jerked back, straining her neck. Thick raindrops pelted her face. She wiped the wetness away and blinked as lightning flared with blinding brightness. She was in her room again, sitting in the same position she had been in when she had left it.

Gray clouds covered the sky now, and large puddles formed on the floor in front of her window. How long had she been away? She took a deep breath and another, excitement mixing with her nausea. She swung her legs over the side of her bed, stood, and splashed barefoot through the water under her window. Rain hit her as she reached outside for the shutters and brought them together, closing out the storm.

Her hands trembled, success stirring inside her. She let out a victorious squeal. She had seen where the Atrox lived. There was another entrance to Hades by way of the Taenarus cave near Marmari in southern Peloponnese. Already her mind raced with plans. She grasped her talisman. The stone vibrated again, demanding the release of its power. The complex grid of letters had returned. Did that mean her plan would succeed?

She was the predator now. She was going to hunt the Atrox. She smiled, imagining what she would do. When she found it in its lair, she'd recite the incantation before it could flee. Her smile fell away as another thought came to her, but she refused to allow herself to consider what would happen to her when she spoke the words etched into the stone out loud.

Lightning streaked across the sky outside, its white light filtering through the shutters. Thunder crashed, vibrating around her.

Determined, Penelope went downstairs to find her father. She didn't feel the presence of the Atrox now, and she wanted to speak with him before she went away.

He was sitting alone in the *andron*, bowls of olives and cheese untouched in front of him. A single wick burned in the corner, fluttering and ready to go out. He stared at the floor, holding a cloak that had belonged to Taemestra. He glanced up, and from his expression she knew he no longer saw her as an innocent girl.

"I'm leaving to go down to Tartarus," she said, in a voice that brooked no argument. "I have to stop the Atrox before more people are harmed."

Wind screamed around the house, thunder jolting the walls.

"Do you want me to go with you?" her father asked.

His words were not what she had expected. She had assumed he would try to stop her.

"No," she answered. "I'll go alone."

"Are you going to help your sister?" He made a sound as if there were tears caught in his throat.

She nodded. "I'll try."

"I saw her," he said in a battle-weary voice that implied he had seen too much. "She was alive, but dead. Her eyes were no longer Taemestra's. I tried to stop the men with her, but a sword can't kill a shade. How will you stop it?"

She clutched her amulet and swallowed hard, wondering if she could. Was it possible?

"I always knew you'd choose a difficult path," he said at last.

"Has it always been my destiny?" she asked slowly. "Or was it Hera's curse on me for being Zeus's bastard child?"

He sighed. "Yes, Zeus is your real father."

"Zeus may have seduced my mother and created me, but my real father is the man who stood by me day after day and cared for me," Penelope said firmly.

Her father's eyes filled with appreciation and love, but then he added, "Don't anger Zeus. He's the great father of us all."

After a long pause, Penelope took a deep breath. "I want you to pour the libations for me as I've done for you so many times."

He stood. "We'll need to make a greater sacrifice."

Hours later, the clouds had scattered and the sound of dripping water was the only reminder of the storm. Penelope and her father walked through the Doric colonnade of the unfinished temple of Zeus. Many of the column drums had been broken down and used to build the city walls, but her father favored this temple as a place to gain Zeus's attention.

A priest stood in front of a fire. Nine attendants led a white bull to him. The priest washed his hands and sprinkled water on the bull. Then her father scattered grain, and as the bull ate, the priest cut its throat with a single slashing blow.

Penelope winced and dug her face into her father's chest, unable to watch the attendants skin the beast and cut it into pieces. At last the priest wrapped the thighbones in rich fat and set them on the fire. Smoke churned to the heavens.

Then her father raised his hands to the sky and prayed. "Mighty Zeus, king of the deathless gods, lord of thunder and lightning bolt, if ever you have been pleased with the rich smoke of my sacrifice, hear me now. Protect our daughter Penelope."

Winds lashed around the fire, and the priest gave them a look that told them Zeus was pleased.

Her father cleared his throat as if he were trying to hold back tears. He seldom showed affection in public, but he grabbed her now, wrapping his huge arms around her.

"I've always loved you as my own daughter," he spoke quickly. "Now I pray to mighty Zeus to bestow his blessings on you and give you his divine protection."

His words were said to calm and comfort her, but the tone sounded as if he were standing at her grave, saying his final good-bye.

CHAPTER TWENTY

DAYS INTO HER journey, Penelope walked along the edge of a gorge. Wind blustered around her, and the setting sun cast gold over the hill. She followed a goat trail, winding down between briar and boulders to the sea. Thorns and cockleburs snagged her tunic, but even the raw blisters stinging her feet didn't slow her. She needed to reach the beach before dusk. She couldn't bear another night curled in a dank-smelling cave on the cliff.

The trail forked ahead of her. She had stepped onto the steeper path when a twig

snapped behind her. She paused. Pebbles spat-
tered and bounced from the ledge overhead.
Someone was following her, and whoever it was
wasn't bothering to hide his approach. But why
should he? She was alone. There was no place to
run. She had wondered why the Atrox hadn't
pushed into her mind, and now she knew. It had
sent Followers instead, to stop her and punish her
for her deception.

She slipped behind a pile of rocks and waited.

Soon a man walked down the hill, his coarse
wool cloak and long hair breezing behind him.
He carried a red shield painted with the enemy
mark of Sparta.

His eyes looked lost in thought, not dead
like a Follower's. Maybe he was trailing behind
her with a plan to kidnap her. She'd soon find
out. She scaled a boulder and crouched, ready to
spring, then jumped, using surprise and her
falling body to tackle him to the ground.

He pitched forward and hit the rocky path
with a thump, his forehead grazing a boulder. A
groan escaped his lungs and his shield banged

down the cliff. She straddled his back and yanked his sword from its scabbard. The gleaming metal flashed the last rays of the sun. He rolled beneath her, trying to throw her from his back, turned, and stopped his struggling, his surprise obvious.

"A girl?" He started to laugh.

She took advantage of his moment of hesitation to place the blade tip against his throat. His hands fell into the dust.

"Why are you following me?" She stared into his eyes, his candid face weathered from the sun. "No lies."

"I was longing for companionship," he said. He wasn't much older than she was, but that didn't mean he wasn't full of deceit.

She dug her knees into his ribs and let the blade slip in. A trickle of blood ran down his sunburned skin. She wasn't going to be fooled. Not now, when she was so close. "You could have told a better story than that."

His chest heaved beneath her. With a start she realized he was crying. It had to be a ruse. Spartan boys were reared from childhood to be ruthless and aggressive warriors. They weren't even given enough food to eat in order to force them to learn how to forage and steal.

"My brother was killed," he said at last. "I'm going to Hades to thank his shade for saving my life and to ask his forgiveness for not giving him a proper burial."

"You were defeated in battle?" She hoped that if her father had been involved he was safe, but then her fury rose. "Why do men insist on war? Your brother would be with you now if you could live in peace."

He shook his head as if his lifetime of training had lost its meaning. "I don't know what I'll do. I can't go home. You cannot understand, because you're from Athens."

"How do you know?" she asked, surprised, and immediately her suspicion mounted. Was he trying to distract her? Were others on the trail? She couldn't afford to look behind her, but now she wondered if she had been tricked. He didn't seem like a Follower, but that didn't mean he wasn't working with them.

"You look pampered," he said at last.

Their eyes locked.

"Pampered?" She started to argue but stopped.

New tears ran down his cheeks. He was deep in mourning, his grief reminding her of her own losses.

"Why can't you go home?" she asked softly, keeping the sword pressed against his neck.

His wet eyes searched the darkening sky. "In Sparta, mothers prefer to have their sons die in battle rather than come home in defeat. It's better if my mother believes she has lost both sons than for her to have to endure the shame of having me return home."

His answer didn't seem reasonable. "A mother's love would overcome anything."

"Maybe in Athens—," he started.

"Tell me the real truth," she interrupted, and raised the sword high. "Why are you following me?"

He didn't answer and she didn't have a choice. She had to kill him or be killed. She couldn't trust him even if he wasn't in league with the Followers. If she let him go, he would turn on her. He was large, his muscles trained. He could throw her over the cliff. At best he'd sell her as a slave. Her heart pounded; she didn't know what to do.

"I welcome death," he whispered, and didn't move. "Kill me and tell everyone you killed the warrior Chrysippus."

CHAPTER TWENTY-ONE

CHRYSIPPUS HAD remained still, but Penelope couldn't kill him. She had stepped off him, dropping the sword, and waited until his racking sobs had ended. He hadn't cried from relief but in defeat. In the end she had convinced him to go with her. She needed his Spartan courage but even after traveling with him for two days the memory of that first night still surprised her. They had spent it sleeping curled together, in brambles and vines like two runaway orphans.

Now he pulled flat bread from under his tunic, tore off a piece, and handed it to her. He took a bite from the loaf and stared, mesmerized, at the entrance to a nearby cave.

"We should be starting down soon." Penelope bit into the hard bread. A sour, bitter taste nettled her tongue. She spit. "This is terrible." She studied the scrap still in her hand. Gray-green mold spotted it.

"You're too finicky." Chrysippus grabbed back the portion he had given her, but before he could chuck it into his mouth, she pinched it from his fingers and tossed it to the sparrows.

"You shouldn't waste food." He looked dismayed.

The birds flew down, twittering, pecked at the lump of bread, then twitched their heads sideways and flew away.

"See, even the birds refuse to eat it," she said. "Because it's disgusting."

He picked the bread from the dirt and pushed it into his mouth. "Spartans don't eat for taste like Athenians. We need food only for nourishment."

He smirked. "You've never had to scrounge for food. I have. I told you. You're pampered."

Penelope shook her head and laughed, then caught the shadows lurking in the cave. Her light mood fell away, replaced with an ominous feeling of dread. She stood and clasped her talisman. "We'd better start."

Chrysippus joined her and placed his red cloak around her, the rough wool scratching her shoulders. "It'll be cold inside."

He stepped forward and the darkness swallowed him. She followed the scuffing sound of his sandals, her hands brushing along the crusty cavern walls.

As they went deeper, fear began prickling through her body. Why had she ever thought she could sneak up on the Atrox? Her plan seemed foolish now. What kind of pride made her believe she could destroy something that people had been fighting for centuries without success?

A dull green glow rose from the churning mists and the gaseous air choked with a sulfur stench.

They continued in silence for hours, winding

down the narrow path; then Chrysippus broke the quiet with a sharp intake of breath. She stepped next to him and looked over the edge of a cliff. Below them, hundreds of ghost soldiers, covered with blood and dirt, wandered aimlessly on the vast shores of the river Styx. Some still had arrows and spears sticking through them.

"There must have been a terrible battle," Penelope said.

"The one I was in." Chrysippus started down the slope, his eyes searching the vaporous shades. "They'll be unable to cross to the other shore, because none of them were given proper burials." He untied a coin from the hem of his tunic. "But I'll give this obol to Charon to pay my brother's passage."

Suddenly Chrysippus cried in joy and ran across the beach, spectral shapes fluttering around him. He tried to embrace his brother but couldn't grasp his phantom body. "Dexileos, if you hadn't been trying to save me, you'd still be alive, not here."

Dexileos moved his lips, but only a dry whistle came out.

"He needs blood to speak." Penelope joined them, the dead whispering around her, eager for a remembrance of life, their diaphanous forms whisking over her like spiderwebs.

Chrysippus drew his sword, sliced his palm, and held up his bleeding wound for his brother to drink. Ghosts pressed around him, murmuring and whining, trying to lick a drop of blood.

Dexileos drank and then he spoke. "Why is this girl with you?" The power of his gaze made Penelope step back. "Does she have a relative here?"

"We're going down to Tartarus to fight the Atrox," Chrysippus answered. "Do you know which path to take?"

"I should have refused your blood." He elongated himself and quavered, seeming overcome with fear. Could the Atrox reach into death and harm a person's shade?

"The Atrox is gone," he said at last. "Don't look for it here or anywhere. It's her destiny, not yours."

Chrysippus didn't argue with his brother;

instead he held up the coin, stepped to the lapping waters, and gave the money to Charon who stood on the stern of his boat holding a punt pole.

"Take my brother to the other shore," Chrysippus said.

Charon took the coin and Dexileos glided on board. Then Charon dipped his pole into the muddy water and pushed away from shore, the water splashing lazily.

A strange sureness came over Penelope as the boat disappeared into mists. The Atrox had been watching her all along, taking its time. She wasn't the huntress but the prey. She looked at the shifting shadows, knowing somewhere the Atrox waited for her.

CHAPTER TWENTY-TWO

PENELOPE BURST FROM the gloomy cavern into sunlight, gasping and taking deep gulps of fresh air. Only then did she realize how frightened she had become on their trek back. She glanced at Chrysippus. The veins in his neck pulsed as if his heart were exploding in his chest.

She took his hand, feeling the fine tremor in his fingers. "Go home to your mother," she whispered. "Your brother's right. This is my battle, not yours."

"I'm only shivering from the cave's cold." He wrenched his hand back. "There was nothing to fear inside."

"Penelope!" Someone called her name.

She whirled around. Taemestra ran across a field of yellow flowers, stirring butterflies and grasshoppers, her torn tunic flapping around her legs. A scarf twisted her hair up and away from her face. She looked as if she had journeyed many days.

Penelope backed away, but Taemestra threw her arms around her and hugged her. "I've been searching for you ever since Father told me you were going to save me." She caught her breath. "Can you ever forgive me for what I've done?"

Penelope glanced at Taemestra, her chest tightening with anger. "What do you want?"

"Help me," Taemestra went on. "I don't want to be a Follower anymore."

"How can I believe you?" Penelope hesitated, a terrible sick feeling flooding through her. She wanted to trust her sister, but she couldn't stop staring into Taemestra's dead, blank gaze. Could a Follower have a change of heart?

Taemestra worked the scarf in her hair, unwrapping it. "I knew you wouldn't believe me unless I proved myself." Her lush curls fell free, and something dropped to the ground with a thump.

Penelope picked it up and stared at the moonstone that had been stolen from the temple of Selene. Her hands quivered as she held it up to the sun and examined it. A flaw in the middle had the shape of a woman. "How did you get this?"

"I stole it back from the Atrox." Taemestra looked clearly afraid, as if a shadow might be hovering nearby and listening.

Penelope tied the moonstone into one of the tattered shreds of her own tunic.

"Please." Taemestra touched her shoulder; her lifeless eyes had gathered tears.

"All right," Penelope said. "We'll try to find a way to free you."

But when she opened her arms to embrace Taemestra, Chrysippus thrust his hand between them.

"If she's still in league with the Atrox," Chrysippus said, "then it could have given her the stone to make you trust her."

"I risked everything to steal it," Taemestra argued.

"Then show us where the Atrox is hiding," Chrysippus challenged.

"I'll show you," Taemestra whispered, her face pale and tense.

After a pause she turned and trudged through a field, Penelope close beside her, dry grass crackling beneath their feet. Chrysippus lagged behind, his eyes wary.

A startled rabbit dashed in front of them. It scurried away, then stopped, turned abruptly, hind paws scattering dust and twigs, and charged back, dashing wildly around their legs. Whatever it had encountered was more frightening to it than the three of them.

"What scared it?" Penelope asked, looking after the rabbit with wonder.

"Look." Chrysippus pointed.

Heat waves undulated over the meadow

ahead, and the fiery sun cast an odd glimmer over blackened trees, rocks, and cactus. A crow soared into the sky, its glossy wings spread wide. Its feathers looked as sharp as blades, long and pointed as if it wore armor.

"What is this place?" Penelope stepped forward, and a strange tingling crawled over her skin.

Violets, hyacinths, and crocuses grew in the grass, petals spiking, their sweet fragrance a miasma. The husks of dead butterflies ruffled in the breeze beneath the blossoms.

"We're near where the Atrox dwells," Taemestra said. Her beautiful face seemed cut into angles now. She halted at the edge of a pit. "Here's the entrance to the bottom of the world."

Penelope and Chrysippus stared into the unimaginably deep hole. The walls were dead vertical with jagged projections sharp enough to cut flesh.

"A man could fall for a year and not touch bottom," Penelope whispered, repeating what Er had told her.

"We'll find the Atrox here." Taemestra

picked up coils of weathered rope. The ends were tied around the trunk of a tree. She threw them over the edge. They tangled like a nest of snakes.

"The void is deeper than the ropes are long," Penelope said. "What good will they do us?"

"You don't need to go all the way down," Taemestra explained. "There are tunnels cut into the sides."

"Is this the way Followers get down?" Chrysippus freed a rope, tested it, and stood too close to the edge. Pebbles and rocks clattered down the side but never made the sound of hitting bottom.

"Followers become shadows and fly," Penelope explained.

Disbelief flickered in his eyes, then disappeared. His clenched his jaw and started down. "I'll take the first tunnel I reach."

Penelope held her rope taut, then eased onto the rim, clumps of dirt breaking free. She leaned back, braced her feet against the gritty wall, and dropped into the unknown darkness below. She had only gone a little way when soft thunder filled the shaft, vibrating through her.

A boulder fell and skimmed her shoulder. Pain raced through her arm and she was knocked off balance. Her feet lost their hold and she swung away from the cavern wall. The rope creaked, threads unwinding.

"Taemestra!" She tried to see her sister, but stones and pebbles rumbled over her, drumming against the outcroppings. She bent her head, legs, and arms clinging to the rope.

"I'm in here," Chrysippus yelled from a hole in the side of the cavern. "Try to swing to me."

She pumped her body and the rope swung. Chrysippus grabbed her arm, yanked her to him, and pulled her into the mouth of a cave as the rope snapped and tumbled down.

"But Taemestra," Penelope cried. "We have to help her."

She strained to see her sister. Dust cleared and what she saw made her heart stop. Taemestra and the two men who had helped her before were pushing boulders over the unstable ledge. The side of the shaft slumped and unleashed an avalanche. Earth and debris roared down on them.

Chrysippus drew her back. "Come in to safety!"

"Safety?!" she answered. "We're going to be buried alive."

CHAPTER TWENTY-THREE

PENELOPE STUMBLED deeper into the cave. A storm of dust and sand howled after her, pursuing her down the tunnel with the promise of death. Pebbles snapped from the cloud, striking her back and legs. More stones skimmed across the rock floor, hitting her feet at impossible speed. She stretched her hands in front of her, silt clogging her nose, and ran blindly, tripping and staggering, trying to stay with Chrysippus.

Rolling dirt chased after them for a long time, the fury of the landslide shuddering through the cavern walls; then it was gone. The rumbling stopped and the earth settled with sporadic trembles and quakes.

"Are you all right?" Chrysippus asked, and cleared his throat.

"Yes," she answered with a cough. Her feet ached and her thighs burned, but her lungs had begun to work again. She drew in long breaths of dank fetid air and became aware of the sound of dripping water. She brushed her hands behind her. Her fingers jammed against cold wet rock and moss. She sipped from the dribbling spring and spit, trying to clear her mouth of powdery dirt.

Something brushed against her arm. Her head snapped around. "Was that you, Chrysippus?"

"What?" He wheezed, his voice still too far away. He couldn't have touched her.

She rubbed her skin, trying to wipe away the strange sensation, when something fluttered over her again like a tickle of feathered wing and then it was gone.

"I think a bird is trapped with us." She waved her hand through the air, but if something had been in the darkness with them, it was gone now.

"A bird couldn't have survived the avalanche," he said. "And if it had, it would be chirping."

"You're right," she answered. Maybe dust sliding down her arm had created the odd sensation of someone's touch. "What do we do now?"

"We follow the tunnel and find another way out." Chrysippus grappled in the dark, kicking stones. His fingers touched her face, then found her hand. "Your sister said the tunnels lead to the same place."

"Let's go, then," she said, but an uneasy feeling had taken hold.

They started forward with deliberate, slow steps.

She blinked, trying to adjust her eyes to the dark, but in the blank hollow of the cave sight was of no use to her. Then, from the corner of her eye, she sensed movement. She turned and stared at a shadow darker than the blackness surrounding her. It streaked toward her and curled up her arm, as soft as smoke. She wrenched back and tried to brush it away.

"What is it?" Chrysippus asked sharply.

"I saw something," she whispered, hating the fear in her voice.

"You can't see anything," Chrysippus answered, his voice determined. His hand found her shoulder and squeezed it with reassurance.

"But I felt it." She touched her dust-coated skin again.

"Dirt," he answered. "It's making my skin crawl, too. I need a bath."

"Maybe." Her fingers found his arm, his warmth giving her comfort, but her stomach clenched when she looked back at the black void. It was as it had been, completely empty now, but she was certain she had felt something more.

"Let's go," he said.

She started advancing again, feet shuffling over the craggy floor, but then on impulse she glanced over her shoulder. A dusky cloud ran across her field of vision. Something had been following stealthily that didn't want to be seen.

"Chrysippus." She pulled on his arm.

Behind them a stone clicked as if someone had been walking and stopped.

"It's only the ground still settling," he assured her.

"But I saw——" A soft mewling made her pause. She frowned and inched closer to him. "Did you hear that?"

"Something. It sounds like people imprisoned in the stones." His voice fell away as the whimper came again, soft and muffled. "It has to be some illusion caused by trickling water and the deepness of the earth."

She let go of Chrysippus and patted her palms across the wet and mossy cavern wall, hoping to perceive the vibration of a river roaring underground, but it lay still beneath her hands and she couldn't feel the source of the sound. "No, it's not from the water. Something's in the tunnel with us."

"Look back," Chrysippus said suddenly. Metal rubbed against leather as he slipped his sword from its sheath. The blade clanked softly against rock.

With dreamlike slowness she turned. Swirling patterns of black swept toward them, rustling over each other and forming menacing faces.

"Shadows need light," she said. "How do we see them?"

"We're in a different world." Chrysippus stood close beside her, his breath falling against her shoulder. He wrapped one arm around her as if he could protect her from the phantoms that surged and grew. "Maybe they're not shadows but some demon form of ghost."

The silhouettes joined together and raced down the tunnel, screaming with an almost human voice. The cry shuddered through her.

Chrysippus pushed her behind him. She fell against the rock, scraping her cheek, then turned as his sword sliced through the dark with a whipping sound. It swished again, and then the blade scraped against stone; its clanging echoed, and sparks flew in the air.

The shadows rolled over each other, spurring each other forward, their whispers bubbling with glee as if the creatures had been energized and pleased with his attack.

"My sword went through them," Chrysippus said with obvious astonishment; then reason returned. "I must have missed them. I won't this time."

A sudden primitive instinct rose in her, the sensation so strong she was sure of what she was saying. "Don't fight them." She clasped his arm; his muscles were hard and tight as he gripped the sword for another assault. "We only make them stronger if we fight them. We need to turn and walk away."

"Walk away?" His tone told her he thought her idea an insult.

She pulled on him. "They're connected to the Atrox somehow."

"Its sentinels?" he asked. "Maybe we're close and they guard it."

"I don't know. Sheath your sword." Beneath her fingers his arm relaxed as if he sensed the truth in what she was saying.

His sword slipped into its scabbard with a rasping sound.

The shadows drew back, irritated, dark points watching the way a cat observes its weakened prey before it pounces for the last time. A single tendril whipped out like a paw, goading them to attack.

"They're going to kill us," Chrysippus said, but she didn't detect any fear in his voice, only resignation. "Continue down the tunnel. I'll slow them. Maybe there's a way for you to escape at the other end."

"Not without you." She tugged on his arm. "Let's go. Now."

He remained motionless; even his breathing was silent. "What do they want with us? If we knew, then maybe we could find a way to defeat them."

"They wants *us*, our life force," she whispered. "But I have a plan."

"What?" he asked.

"Run!" She turned and sprinted, dragging him with her, plunging headlong into the dead blank world in front of her.

Shadows swirled around them, seeping

between them as if trying to pull them apart. She struggled to breathe and slammed into jutting rocks. Pain shot through her, then she pushed back and continued moving faster than before, stubbing her toes on stones.

"It must be the black cloud of Thanatos," he said, rushing behind her. "That's the only way we can see it in this darkness."

"Death doesn't want to kill us," she argued between frantic gulps for air. "The shadows belong to the Atrox."

"They say death travels in a mist of darkness," he argued, gaining on her. "We must have died in the landslide and it's only now come for us."

"We're alive!" she shouted.

"Why go on?" he asked, but she didn't detect fear in his voice, only rage. "We're the innocent victims of the gods."

He stopped. "This is because of me," he said, and started toward the shadows as if defeated. "My death is required to atone for the demise of my brother."

"It's not!" She yanked him back.

Something slithered across the dark, and for a moment she felt it pressing against her, twisting cold and hungry around her, stealing her warmth. She began to shiver.

"I want to live." She jerked his arm, frantic. "Help me. Then you can sit down and die."

He took her hand, urged on, and this time he led her, running wildly, his feet crushing over broken rocks, but then, without warning, he stopped with a loud *thwack* and groaned. She collided with him, her chin hitting the top of his head.

He sprawled on the ground. "This end of the tunnel has also caved in."

"It can't be." Her hands flew into the air, waving frantically, searching for an opening. Her knuckles smacked against rock and two of her fingernails tore free on a spiking stone.

"We're at the end of the tunnel," he said softly.

Exhausted, she crumpled beside him, her fingers exploring his face. A bruise was swelling on his cheek, and warm blood trickled from his mouth.

"It's time now," he whispered and settled his arm around her. "We tried."

The shadows fixed on them with evil hunger.

She shuddered. "I can't die now. There's too much I haven't done yet."

His soft breath was on her cheek, his fingers tenderly turning her face to his. "If we must die now, let's do so feeling love, not fear."

She let him pull her against his body, sighing as their lips met.

Suddenly the wall behind them crashed inward with an earsplitting boom. The thunderclap reverberated through the cavern, jolting the walls. Boulders spun past them, and a blinding light shattered the dark.

Penelope blinked and peeked through her fingers, her eyes stinging from the sudden brightness. The silhouette of a huge man filled the gaping hole. He stomped forward, grabbed Chrysippus, and threw him across the cavern.

Then his hands reached down and grasped Penelope.

CHAPTER TWENTY-FOUR

HECTOR HELD PENELOPE tight against him, his face livid, eyes bright pools of fire. She could feel an evil aura surrounding her, but she also sensed his love. "What was he doing to you?"

"Nothing," she said, still stunned and feeling dizzy from the sudden light.

Chrysippus lay slumped over rocks, blood on his chin. He shook his head, then jumped up, swung his sword into the air, and silently stepped forward, his eyes narrowed in concentration.

Hector pushed Penelope aside and drew his own sword, his expression eager.

"He's not my enemy," Penelope yelled. "And he wasn't hurting me. It was a kiss good-bye. We thought we were going to die."

Hector glanced at her, his eyes now as she remembered them. He seemed overcome with emotion and let his sword fall. He took her hand.

A flurry of questions came to her, and at the same time she wondered how she could still want Hector so desperately. "How did you escape? Are you all right?"

"There's no time!" Chrysippus yelled. "They're coming."

Hector quickly turned around and studied the dark shaft behind them; then he looked back at Penelope, his voice urgent. "You must willingly go with me."

Penelope felt herself plunging into a whirlwind of emotions. As much as she loved Hector, how could she trust him now? He was bound to the Atrox. Maybe he was sent here to trick her? Or worse, destroy her?

"Yes, take us," Chrysippus yelled, before she could answer.

Then she glanced up and saw what he had been looking at. The unnatural shadows swept toward them, shrieking and whipping through the air, their black fury pledging a fate worse than death.

"What are they?" she asked, fear ripping through her.

"They're the shadow demons who carried me from the underworld and cast me from earth into the night skies," Hector answered, his gaze filled with hate.

Her survival instinct overrode all other thoughts. "Take us. Now!"

Hector grasped their hands and the air began to shimmer, his hold tightening. A powerful force shuddered through Penelope, making the fine hairs on the back of her neck stand on end; then her body felt as if it were being pricked by thorns.

Chrysippus let out a whistle of air as if he felt it, too.

Was Hector taking them to the stars? In

panic she wondered what it would be like to wander as he did through the heavens. Her hands began to tremble and her heartbeat raced.

A suffocating pressure tightened around them and then Chrysippus yelled.

She looked down and saw what had frightened him. They were dissolving. Their hands looked like swarming gnats. A scream skidded up her throat, but before it reached her mouth, she was gone.

CHAPTER TWENTY-FIVE

BLACK SPECKS WRITHED in the air around Penelope. Then, with a start, she realized it was her body trying to become whole again. Where had Hector taken them? Slowly she came back together, and her feet thumped on a marble floor. For a moment, pain spun inside her, and then it was gone. She drew in long, gasping breaths, trying to settle her quivering stomach. At last her eyes focused.

She was in a world far away from the rule of

the gods, closer to death than life. She stood in front of a pool of clear water. Pink, red, and yellow roses climbed up the white, glistening walls of buildings rising behind cascading fountains and filled the air with sweet fragrance.

"Are you all right?" Hector touched her tenderly.

She rubbed her hand down her arm, her skin still prickling. "What did you do to us?"

"To get you away, I had to make you both invisible."

"Invisible?" Chrysippus spoke as if he had a lump in his throat he couldn't swallow; then he turned quickly, checking to see if the shadows had followed them. "Are we still within the bottom of the world?"

"You're safe here," Hector said.

Penelope looked at Chrysippus. He was covered with dirt. Then she glanced down at her own scratched and filthy arms, her black-rimmed jagged nails. She touched her dirt-caked hair. It felt like clumps of clay. She glanced back at the shimmering, turquoise water.

Suddenly not caring, she untied the moonstone from her bedraggled tunic and then, clasping the gem tight in her hand, she dodged behind a rosebush, tore off her filthy clothes and ran into the pool, splashing until she reached its depths. She stayed under for as long as she could, feeling sand and dust wash away, then surged to the surface and swam under the fountains, luxuriating in the perfume of roses.

When she came out at last, Hector stood at the edge, holding a new tunic spread wide for her to wear. He was forcing himself to look away, to give her privacy. She walked slowly toward him, making up her mind about what she would do.

"Where's Chrysippus?" she asked when she reached him and put the tunic on.

"Sleeping over there," he said, staring into her eyes.

Her emotions mixed violently. Did she dare? He had sacrificed everything for her, trying to free her from her vows, and now again he had risked his all to save her from the shadows. "What will the Atrox do to you when it discovers you've escaped?"

"It doesn't matter," he whispered. "I'm with you now."

She started to speak, but he traced a gentle finger over her lips to quiet her, then wrapped his arms around her, pulling her closer.

Her breath caught as a pleasant chill swept through her.

"Don't tell me the reasons we can't be together," he whispered. "I know them all. For all eternity we'll never have more than this one night together."

He kissed her softly, and everything that had happened seemed far away. She let out a soft sigh, enjoying the delicious stirring inside her.

"I love you, Penelope," he whispered. "Be with me tonight."

"I love you, too." She watched his face, entranced by the warmth of his body and the rushing sensations within her own. Her desire was strong and suddenly free.

He swung her into his arms and carried her through a labyrinth of halls and into a room. Small flickering lamp flames cast a golden light across the walls. Incense perfumed the air.

He set her gently on the bed, the many pillows soft beneath her.

She set the moonstone on a small table beside her, then turned back to Hector and took him into her arms.

CHAPTER TWENTY-SIX

P

ENELOPE AWOKE AND sat up quickly, not knowing where she was, then remembered. Hector lay beside her, still sleeping. She breathed in his salty scent and traced a finger over his dark face. She bent to kiss his cheek when a glitter of gold caught her eye. She tugged at the blankets, baring his legs, and stared down at the bands circling his ankles. The serpentine design reflected the flickering lamp flames and seemed to flow sinuously over the metal.

Her heart thundered. Maybe she could free him. She leaned over, searching for a clasp.

Hector jerked his leg away and caught her hand before she could touch the bands. "What are you doing?"

"Trying to free you," she said, looking at him with surprise.

"You can't release me without becoming enslaved yourself." He started to say more, but a change in the air made him stop.

An odd weight settled over them with an ominous feel of impending danger.

She grabbed her tunic, searching the room, and wrapped it around her, tying a knot at her shoulder. "What is it?"

"My evil lord, the Atrox." Hector stood, obviously in pain; the pressure she felt seemed greater on him. He struggled for his sword, his fingers stretching and wrestling with the strange power pressing against him. Finally he gripped the hilt and looked at her with regret. "It's calling me back."

"I thought you had escaped it!" Hurriedly she grasped the moonstone, wrapped it into the tail hem of her skirt, and worked another knot.

"No, it sent me after you."

Fear shuddered through her. "You lied to me."

"You were going to die in the tunnel," he said hoarsely; his jaw locked, and his muscles strained against an immense force.

She understood immediately and ran to him with rising urgency. "The Atrox is trying to stop you from telling me more, isn't it?"

He gasped and his words broke free. "Your sister was supposed to give you the moonstone, then trick you into the tunnel and create the land-slide to imprison you in the Atrox's domain. If it couldn't convince you to join with it, then your only exit would have been through the door that releases the horrors Pandora didn't set free. The moonstone is the only key."

"Pandia told me." She blinked back hot tears. She couldn't lose Hector now, and yet she knew he was leaving. The Atrox throbbed through her, its energy building. It was coming closer. "But why did it send you?"

"The landslide broke down other cavern walls and released the demons the Atrox keeps imprisoned there. You were sealed with them. The Atrox released me to save you and allowed me this one night with you in return. I didn't understand why, but now I see the memory of it will only make me suffer more. How can I exist without you?"

"I feel the same way," Penelope answered. "Death from the demons would have been better than what the Atrox will give me." She looked at the door, expecting it to appear at any moment.

"You have to remember that you are an Immortal now," Hector said. "You would not have died, but you would have suffered." He leaned over her, looking deep into her eyes, and started to kiss her, but when their lips met, his body suddenly became transparent. His sword faded, too.

A soft thunder made her turn. A shadow came at them slowly. Tendrils of smoky cloud curled out, the mists twirling around her feet.

Trembling, she grasped her amulet. "I'll destroy it and free you."

"Don't use the talisman." Hector touched her, his fingers whisking through her. "You'll be gone, and what will I have then?"

She dropped the stone. It thumped against her chest. "I'll find a way to free you. I promise."

"You don't need to destroy yourself to stop the Atrox." His arm moved, shimmering through the air, and he handed her his sword. "Take this and use it."

The sword fell through her fingers, landing at her feet, but as soon as Hector had released it, it pulled together, becoming solid again.

She picked it up. It glimmered with an odd internal light. "Tools of war only make the Atrox stronger."

"Use it! You can escape back to the world of light." His face blurred, lips stretching at an odd angle. "I love you."

"I love you, too." But before she could finish saying the words, he vanished.

Tears obscured her vision. When she blinked them free, the shadowy cloud of the Atrox had spun into a man, black vapors twining around him. It stood in front of her, stepping toward her with slow, easy steps, its eyes filled with the cruel promise of a lasting living death. "So you've come to me."

"No! You brought me here." She concentrated, trying to feel its thoughts, to know what it was planning. She caught a flicker and looked up, surprised.

"You've become a worthy opponent." Its dangerous eyes tried to hold hers.

She grasped the sword and ran from the room, looking for Chrysippus. She had seen how to escape.

The Atrox faded into shadow and stormed after her.

Penelope turned down one corridor after another, running through the interconnecting passages, her footsteps slapping hard against white stone. She spun around the next corner and the next, chasing down the same hallways over and over again.

With a jolt of fear she remembered the stories about the vast underground maze in which the Minotaur had hidden, its victims unable to escape. She had a dreadful feeling that she was only circling until the Atrox decided to end the game.

Frustration overwhelmed her. She had seen how to escape through a tunnel but not how to leave these intertwining corridors. It had seemed so simple when she had dashed from the room. She paused, not knowing what to do.

The Atrox burst angrily into the far end of the hallway, a man's shadow embodied in the center of the storm. She waited for the foul dark to surround her. She no longer had the will or strength left to fight it.

CHAPTER TWENTY-SEVEN

*S*UDDENLY CHRYSIPPUS charged from behind her, sword drawn, and plunged into the roiling mists. He swung hard. The cutting edge pierced the air with a sharp swoosh. The Atrox smiled and folded back into shadow. The blade sliced through seething vapors and hit the stone floor with a loud, echoing crack.

Then, with the fury of a windstorm, the Atrox howled and threw Chrysippus back with tremendous force. He skidded down the corridor, eyelids fluttering, sword clanking end over end, the tip dangerously close to plunging into his stomach.

Penelope dropped Hector's sword and ran to Chrysippus. Falling to her knees, she leaned over him and clutched his hand.

He trembled violently, his face pale. "Go," he said. "Escape while you can. The next doorway will take you back to the pool of water. From there you can find tunnels leading out."

"I'll help you stand, and we'll go together," she said, and glanced over her shoulder at the screaming nightmare cloud.

"Leave me." Chrysippus gasped. "I'll be able to go home on my shield in honor."

"I won't leave you," Penelope answered angrily.

"Then do something," he ordered.

She followed his gaze. The storm had shifted, and the Atrox as a man stepped from its center, eyes gleaming with wretched darkness, footsteps impossibly silent. The air crackled with its presence.

"Now at last I have you." Its hand struck

out and she flinched, but when it touched her with the softness of a night breeze, she stood.

Her fear dissolved, and even the sulfurous stench didn't seem so repugnant now.

Chrysippus said something, but his words faded away.

Glossy black mists swirled lazily around her, caressing her cheeks and arms. The Atrox looked at her with burning eyes, and all her struggles and worries seemed unimportant now. A smile crossed her lips, and her last bit of resistance let go. Why was she trying to escape this beautiful place anyway when she could dwell here forever and have her every whim granted?

"All you have to do is use the moonstone to open the door and release more troubles on the world." The words came, enticing.

She nodded, feeling ashamed that she hadn't thought of it herself. The Atrox and its Followers couldn't open the door because they were evil. But she could. It had always been her destiny.

"Open the door," she whispered, and stared dreamily into the Atrox's dark smoldering eyes.

A yell startled her. She stumbled back, the trance broken. She shook her head.

Chrysippus yelled at her again. "The sword. Use my sword."

The words burst into her awareness. Confusion rattled through her. She couldn't use violence. Chrysippus tossed it to her, hilt first, but she let it clatter onto the floor. She suddenly remembered the sword Hector had given her, but where had she left it?

She turned around, trying to see through the murky haze. At last she spied it, an impossible distance away. She could already feel the Atrox, working into her mind, its hypnotic voice, telling her to turn and come back to it.

Gathering all her strength, she lunged forward, swept the heavy gray sword into her hands, then, holding it in both hands, swung it over her head.

The Atrox seemed amused, its eyes flaunting triumph. "You'll only make me stronger if you strike me. Try."

She hesitated, then suddenly lurched forward. She trusted Hector, loved him, and the Atrox had stolen him from her. She let out all her pent-up feelings in a vicious scream and plunged the sword down.

Fierce magic exploded up her arms, the force of the impact grinding through her with horrific pain. The stone blade flashed a brilliant white light and sliced diagonally into the creature's right shoulder down to where its heart would lie if it had had one.

The Atrox didn't seem hurt, but when she tried to pull the sword free to strike again, it remained immovable, the stone blade fusing with flesh and binding the Atrox to its nimbus of deadly shadow. Desperation slid across its cold yellow eyes, and its evil smile turned into a grimace. It glared at her with fiery hate and thrashed against the blade, slamming back and forth, screaming, a look of horror crossing its arrogant face.

Then she understood. She had fulfilled her real destiny. Pandia had wanted her to bind the Atrox to its shadow to stop it from taking human form, and now she had with the magic Hector had given her.

"Chrysippus!" she yelled, wanting nothing more than to leave this horrible place at the bottom of the world.

The blade burst into fire, melting flesh. The skin began to dissolve, turning back to shadow, but where the sword had entered, thick black blood began to ooze from the wound as if the fiendish cloud were bleeding. Blood seeped around her feet, the carrion stench so strong it made her eyes water.

"Chrysippus," she called again, suddenly fearful something had happened to him.

She stumbled through the roiling angry mists and found him, leaning against the wall, his sword back in its sheath.

"You've defeated it," he said, a new bruise on his arm and an exhausted smile on his face.

"No," she answered, feeling a terrible urgency to leave. "I've only stopped it from taking human form again. The Atrox hasn't been destroyed." As she spoke, cold blood flowed around her feet like an evil quicksand, tugging at her with incredible energy. "Quickly. The Atrox is weak now, but I can feel it gaining strength."

"But you've won." Chrysippus hobbled against her, trying to work through the pain in his ankle.

"We're not safe." She put her arm around him and started toward the end of the hall. "If we don't get away soon, we'll merge with it."

She wasn't sure how she knew, and then with a start she realized she had been reading its thoughts. She glanced back at the black murky liquid following them and shuddered, wondering what kind of endless suffering it carried.

CHAPTER TWENTY-EIGHT

PENELOPE SQUIRMED through the small tunnel, dry earth scraping her side. She took long breaths, trying to get enough air into her lungs, anxiety that she might become trapped mounting inside her. She forced herself to go on.

"Are you sure this is the tunnel that will lead us to the outside world?" Chrysippus asked from behind her.

"This is the one I read in the Atrox's

thoughts," she answered, but doubt was beginning to build.

Suddenly the crawling space became wider. She lifted her head, hoping she could stand, and banged it on the ceiling. Debris fell into her hair.

"Be more careful," Chrysippus ordered. "The land's not stable and the tunnel could collapse."

"I hate the dark," she said, on the verge of tears. "If we escape from here, I'm never going to be without light again."

"If we survive this," Chrysippus said, "I'm going to join you and dedicate my life to fighting the Atrox."

She inched forward, dragging herself into the pitch black in front of her, and then her hands reached out and took hold of nothing. She gasped and her stomach clenched.

Chrysippus clutched the back of her toes. "Why did you stop?"

"We've come to the end," she said, trying to keep her voice steady so he wouldn't detect her defeat and exhaustion.

He squirmed up beside her, squeezing over

her, then shoved her aside until they were pressed shoulder to shoulder. He scraped up a handful of dirt and threw it over the side. Silence followed.

"It must be deep." She tried not to think about the first chasm they had come down on ropes.

"Turn around," Chrysippus ordered.

"Turn around? There's barely room to breathe."

"I'll lower you to the cavern floor," he said. "It can't be more than a few feet."

"You're lying to give me hope," she answered. "What's the real plan?"

"The only path is forward, and if the cave floor is too far below us and we can't find a ledge, then we've met our fate."

"All right." She sighed and let him grab her wrists, then carefully turned, her back scuffing over sharp eruptions of rock. Pebbles slipped beneath her feet.

Finally she eased over the edge, her toes searching for a ridge, anything wide enough to rest her foot on.

"Nothing," she whispered, her last hope crushed.

"I'll bring you back up." He started to pull.

"Why bother?" The feeling had been growing in her. "We can't go back. The only path is forward, remember?"

"You said this was the tunnel," he answered. "There has to be a shelf, something to stand on."

"Chrysippus," she whispered. "The Atrox gave me immortality. If I fall, I will survive."

His silence told her he was thinking, trying desperately to find some plan.

"I would rather fall and spend eternity suffering than let the Atrox hypnotize me again and make me open the door that would set free more horrors on the world." She unwrapped her fingers from his wrists.

"What are you doing?" He tightened his grasp, nails digging into her skin.

"Please," she said. "We have no choice."

"Find a perch for your feet," he ordered angrily. "You didn't try hard enough."

"Release me," she whispered.

"Try again." His rage echoed through the cavern. "There has to be a way we can scale down the cliff."

She swung, toes searching, arms numb from the pressure of his grip, then stopped. "Let me go."

"You have been a true friend," he answered, giving up at last. "I'll join you."

His fingers loosened, and Penelope slipped through his hands, sliding down the rocky slope on her belly.

Her feet landed with a dull thud on solid ground. She tested it with her toe to be sure. She was on a precarious ledge, a path cut into the wall. Happiness surged through her.

Dust rained over her and she looked up. Chrysippus was getting ready to dive into the dark. He'd miss the ledge, she realized, and fall to his death.

"Chrysippus, don't jump!"

CHAPTER TWENTY-NINE

OVERHEAD, CHRYSIPPUS let out a startled cry. A loud *thwack* followed, as if he had lunged back and hit his head on stone.

"It's only a short distance down to the ledge," Penelope yelled up to him. "Slide down the slope so you don't fall into the abyss."

Abrasive, scuffing sounds filled the dark and coarse sand poured over her.

When he reached the outcropping, she held him against her, feeling his thumping heart.

"I almost jumped," he said hoarsely, and caught his breath.

"I know." Then, fighting panic and a fluttering heart, she stepped forward into blackness so thick it looked as if she could scoop it into her hands. She traced her fingers along the wall and tested the ground in front of her with her toes. Each step became a measured calculation.

As they continued down, a sickly sweet odor wafted into the air, growing stronger and more unpleasant in her nose.

Finally the incline leveled. She stretched her toe and felt damp ground surrounding her. "I think we've reached the bottom."

She stepped forward, and her bare foot squished down into thick mud. It oozed between her toes, and the harsh smell became unbearable, making her eyes water and burn. Then something fell on her arm. She batted at it. Another drop fell, and then another. "What is it?"

"Bats!" Chrysippus yelled with joy and grabbed her arms, dancing through the muck. "If bats managed to enter, then there's a way for us to get out."

"This is sickening!" cried Penelope. But happiness surged through her as she sloshed through the thick field of reeking bat guano.

The dimmest light filled the cavern now. Overhead, the ceiling moved. Thousands of bats clung to the limestone, hanging by the claws on the ends of their wings.

Chrysippus screamed. The sound echoed wildly through the vaulting cavern.

The bats unfurled wings and burst around the cave, hundreds of them darting, screeching, and circling.

Penelope threw her hands over her head and waited until they settled back into their roosts, hanging upside-down.

Chrysippus grabbed her hand again, and they ran, laughing, eager to be free.

"The light's coming from crevices overhead," Chrysippus said.

"We can't climb up there." Penelope stared at the dizzying height. "Even if we could, I don't think we'd fit through the openings."

"We'll be able to leave through this tunnel."

Chrysippus yanked her forward and started up a steep incline.

But as she followed, stark unfathomable fear seized her and she stopped. "Something's wrong." She looked around, apprehension working up her spine. "Why isn't the Atrox coming after us?"

He paused, but only for a moment. "You weakened it."

"We're being allowed to leave too easily," she said.

"This has been easy?" He laughed again, but the laughter was forced and nervous this time. His eyes scanned the notched, uneven walls, searching the shadows.

"We haven't escaped," she said. "We've been permitted to go."

"You're imagining things," he said gruffly, and started up the slope.

"Am I?" she asked, trailing behind him, a sickening dread settling in her stomach. "What if we're not being chased because we're doing exactly what it wants?"

Before Chrysippus could answer, she glanced

up, and her heart sank. A massive door stood at the end of the tunnel. She approached it carefully, her senses vibrating, warning her of danger.

Ancient carvings circled the wood. The center was overlaid with gold; part of the design had been obliterated with age, but she could still make out a lion caught in a harness of ropes. Its mouth stretched open in a roar, forming a jewel-encrusted hole.

"It's odd a door should be here." Chrysippus traced his hands over archaic lettering engraved in the stone jamb. "Do you know what this writing says?"

She shook her head. "It's as if someone long ago wrote a curse hoping to frighten away anyone who might open the door."

"It doesn't have a handle or a latch. Maybe it's a wall." He shoved against it, then pulled out his sword and tried to wedge it open.

Penelope grabbed his arm. "Stop."

"Stop?" Sweat beaded his forehead.

"We've been tricked." A horrible sense of foreboding shuddered through her, leaving her hands cold. "The Atrox wants us to open this gateway between two worlds."

"Do you think this is *the* door?" Chrysippus looked unsure.

Her fingers ran over the lion's mouth, and then, with a start, she realized that the hole matched the shape of the moonstone. She untied the knot in her tunic and the stone fell with a thud, its pearly translucence gleaming. She picked it up, and when she did, a strange notion came to her. Taemestra had given her the gem to unlock this door. It was as if the Atrox had seen the future and was helping it along. What would happen if she slipped the sacred moonstone into the jeweled lion's mouth?

"If we open this door," she spoke slowly, sure of what she said, "we'll release unheard of evils and diseases, worse than those from Pandora's box."

He turned and studied the tunnel behind them, his face set and determined.

"We can't save ourselves and let the world suffer," she said. She stepped back, fearful the

Atrox might suddenly appear, entrance her, and make her open the door.

"I don't see anything." Chrysippus sat down, looking suddenly as depleted as Penelope felt. "Just bats."

"Moon legend says a young woman of pure and brave heart will unlock the door." She blushed, but he didn't contradict her self-description. "She'll release the next storm of disease and suffering."

Penelope stared down at the stone clasped in her hand. "Maybe there's another way out."

"We can't climb up to the openings we saw." Chrysippus shook his head, his energy gone. "If you don't open this door, then you've made yourself a prisoner. Maybe the Atrox is counting on your self-sacrifice to keep you here."

"My mentor told me that forces were trying to stop me from taking my vows." Penelope tried to recall everything Pandia had told her. Much of it was a blur now.

"Maybe there's something important you're supposed to do in the future," Chrysippus suggested.

"If there is, and you stay here, then it won't come true."

"But if I unlock the door?" Her words trailed off. What might happen then was too horrifying to contemplate.

"The Atrox wins both ways," Chrysippus said at last. "If we stay, it will have stopped you, and it will still have the moonstone, so it can trick someone else into opening the door."

She had to make a decision, but she faltered, her mind weighing the possibilities. She studied the stone, wishing she knew how to use its dangerous powers. Unexpectedly it began to heat up in her palm. A melodious voice came from it, soft as a sigh of wind, then louder.

Her lips trembled, and she started to shake. Was this another trick the Atrox was playing on her?

"What?" Chrysippus jumped to his feet and stood beside her, gazing at the luminous stone. The flaw inside grew brighter.

"Penelope." The familiar voice spoke her name, bringing back sweet memories of childhood.

"Mother," she whispered, hot tears rushing to her eyes.

Chrysippus placed a comforting hand on her shoulder.

Her head whipped around. For the briefest moment she had thought her mother stood beside her; then she turned back to the stone and placed it against her cheek, listening, feeling its caress of love.

"Hera imprisoned me within the moonstone," her mother whispered. "But Zeus in his pity and love allowed me to remain alive inside until I could speak with you again, on the day you needed me most."

"Then tell me what to do," Penelope begged.

"Things aren't always as they appear," her mother said soothingly. "You must rely on your intuition and trust the greater power inside you to know what to do. You are the daughter of Zeus and have been given an important destiny."

The flaw in the stone faded, and then her mother was gone. Penelope stared at the stone for a long time, her tears falling on its smooth surface. Then, heart hammering, she thrust the stone into the lion's mouth.

A force exploded with blinding light. The door shook violently, then flew open with a blast of thunder. At the same time a boulder crashed behind them, sealing the other entrance. In the gloom, fissures spread across the tunnel walls, snapping and shattering with a deafening clatter.

From deep within foul creatures like wisps of smoke squirmed from the cracks, fuming and thrashing, trying to break free. Awful gurgling sounds came from their stretched-out mouths, and then they began to scream. A volley of discordant cries shook the dim cavern. Demons of inconceivable disaster, warfare, and plague were trying to escape.

Penelope's heart dropped. "What have I done?"

CHAPTER THIRTY

TERRIFIED, PENELOPE grabbed the moonstone from the lion's mouth and ran through the opening to the outside. Chrysippus followed her. Together, they leaned against the door, straining and shoving it with their shoulders, trying to close it.

"It won't budge," Chrysippus yelled.

"I've done something unforgivable," Penelope cried, the terrible fury of the demons vibrating through her. She dropped the moonstone and pushed against the door until her wrists throbbed.

The creatures were far away, but they

shrieked with malice as if they had spied the light. As one they raced toward the door, creating a whirlwind filled with unthinkable promise.

"Use the talisman you told me about!" Chrysippus yelled, his voice harsh.

She grasped the amulet, but there was no reassuring *thrum* in the palm of her hand.

"The power doesn't want to be released," she shouted in disbelief, and stared down, trying to find the incantation inscribed on the amulet; but the letters had hidden themselves inside.

"Is it saving itself for some later day?" Chrysippus slammed his fist against the wood. "What could be more important than this?"

Frustration rose inside her; then, with a shock, she remembered Pandia's instructions.

"A key that can unlock the door can also be used to lock it!" She fell to her knees, her fingers fumbling through grass and weeds. "The moon-stone. Where did I drop it?"

Its clear luminescence reflected the sun. She grabbed it, then searched the outside of the door for a place to set it. Her hands trembled over the splintered wood, but she found nothing, not even a notch.

"There's got to be another hole on this side of the tunnel to lock the door," she said.

"I don't see anything." Chrysippus spread his hands over the top.

The demon winds sped toward them, reeking of death and decay.

She had to do something. She didn't want to be remembered like Pandora.

At last she knew what to do. The only way to find the place to put the stone and lock the portal was to go to the Atrox and search its mind. Did she have the strength? She didn't have a choice. She stepped back, trembling, unable to breathe, and closed her eyes.

"What are you doing?" Chrysippus yelled. "Help me."

Soon his voice slipped far away, and the winds became a distant murmur. She drifted down the thread that bound her to the Atrox, her concentration intense. An odd trancelike feeling tightened around her head and she was falling, wandering through barren emptiness. Abruptly she connected to the Atrox's foul existence. She slid through memories, fascinated and repelled, searching for one in particular. She scanned recollections, then at last saw what she was seeking. Another lion was engraved in the granite skirting block, hidden now behind twisting vines, its mouth roaring wide.

Silently she fell back and skimmed down the telepathic road toward her body.

Then she became aware of something speeding with her. The other presence shivered through her, and then the Atrox seized her, its raw power binding her, its evil humming with a sickening vibration.

I feel your sweet terror, it whispered across her mind.

She remained defiantly still, hoping to find a way to escape, but the Atrox only bound her tighter.

I admire your treachery. The words were a compliment. *Let the disease and sorrows go. Why continue to struggle? Wouldn't it be easier to join me?*

A bit of madness climbed up her mind and nested there, showing her a wonderful existence as a Follower. Why hadn't she understood how good it would be? She found herself desperate to please the Atrox now.

"Let the demons escape," she agreed, eager to win its favor.

With a sharp jolt, she slammed back into her body. She blinked, confused, a moan escaping her lips, then looked down at the moonstone still in her hand and hurled it away.

"Why did you do that?" Chrysippus stood posed at the door with his sword, ready for battle.

She stared down the tunnel, her stomach tight, body stiff, bracing for the onslaught of night creatures swarming at her with frightening speed.

CHAPTER THIRTY-ONE

BUT PART OF Penelope was aware that the Atrox held her, and that part rebelled, straining against the Atrox's hypnotic pull. She fought with her entranced self and worked her fingers free from the mesmerizing hold, then grasped the talisman, its soft vibration now, like a purr, reassuring her. She focused her growing strength through the amulet. The incantation in the stone circled rapidly, buzzing against her palm, and then a terrible burst of power fired through her. She staggered back, nerves throbbing, free.

"What did I do with the moonstone?" she asked, frantic, looking around.

"Over there." Chrysippus pointed, but his eyes remained fixed on the whirling maelstrom almost at the door. "You threw it."

She dashed through weeds and swept it into her hand. It glowed, a spear of light. She ran back and yanked weeds and vines from the rocks, fingers scraping over the rough surface. At last, she found the other lion, etched in the granite block at the base of the door. She slipped the moonstone into its mouth. Fiery sparks shot out with stunning intensity and spiraled around her.

The heavy door slammed shut with a resounding crash. The creatures on the other side hurled themselves against the wood, scratching and pounding and howling to be set free.

"We won." Chrysippus hugged her, his breathing ragged.

"Only for the moment." Slowly she took the moonstone back and tied it in her tunic. "But for now we're safe, and that feels like such a luxury."

* * *

That night after they had bathed in the ocean, Penelope sat on the beach and held the moonstone up to the lunar glow. The flaw in the center was gone now. She hoped that meant her mother had found peace. Then she leaned back against Chrysippus and stared at the night sky.

"I vow to destroy the Atrox someday," she whispered, her longing for Hector unbearable.

"I'm going to help you," Chrysippus answered. "We've already uncovered one secret about it. It can be weakened. I don't think it will be able to take the form of a man again."

She nodded. "For now it's imprisoned in its cloud. Maybe we can uncover other secrets."

They were silent for a while, and then Chrysippus spoke. "Tomorrow you'll start for Athens, but I have no home to go to now."

"I'm not going to stay there. I have to return the moonstone to the temple," she said. "And after that we'll see where the wind takes us. I feel that we're needed, but I don't know where. Maybe the moon will show us."

CHAPTER THIRTY-TWO

PENELOPE AND CHRYSIPPUS got off the boat in Piraeus early in the morning, before the sun had burned away the mists. Already the port was busy with slaves unloading ships, the smells of spices and tar mixing in the air with the fragrance of the sea.

Chrysippus had cut his hair in the fashion of the men of Athens and wore a beard, his red cloak exchanged for a dusky white one they had purchased along the way.

They found a cart and paid the driver to take them into the city. Finally it stopped in front of the temple of Selene.

Inside, Penelope unwrapped the moonstone from her tunic and placed it on the altar.

A hand touched her shoulder. Pandia stood behind her.

Penelope panicked and closed her eyes against the look of distrust and accusation she imagined on Pandia's face. How was she going to explain returning the stone?

"I didn't steal it," she said nervously. "I was only putting it back."

"I never thought you had stolen it." Pandia picked it up and gave it to Penelope. "It belongs to you now."

Penelope stared down at it. "Why are you giving it to me?"

"You're my successor. You're to become the mentor of the Daughters of the Moon. That's why the Atrox has been trying to stop you."

Penelope felt certain she had misunderstood.

Then Pandia handed her a small vial. "This

is an elixir from Selene, to counteract your aging. The potion must be taken during the full moon for its strongest effect, but it can be used at other times. The liquid will regenerate," Pandia explained. "Now I have much to tell you before you leave for Rome."

"Rome?" Penelope felt suddenly dizzy.

"Yes," Pandia went on. "The Daughters there need you. You will be their Magna Mater, their guardian mother."

Suddenly Penelope felt a light from her heart reaching through the ages and connecting with all the Daughters who would come to her, including the one who would one day take her place over two thousand years from now on a continent not yet discovered in a city called Queen of the Angels. The daughters would call her Maggie, for Magna Mater.

Pandia seemed to be showing her all this by some magic. Then she waved her hand and Penelope saw Hector's child growing inside her and the part their child would someday play in the battle.

"It's time to renew your vows," Pandia said at last.

"I have a friend—," Penelope started.

"Bring Chrysippus with you," Pandia answered. "I've been waiting for him."

Breathless, Maggie stopped at the door to her apartment. Her hands smoothed over the wood, feeling the evil waiting for her inside. She closed her eyes now, concentrating on a plan, then pleaded for strength to complete her task.

She had become too careless. There was much more she had needed to tell the Daughters so they would be able to protect themselves. Maybe Chrysippus, now known as Chris, the Keeper of the Secret Scroll, could help them. If not, what would happen when the Atrox discovered the identity of the girl who was supposed to take Maggie's place?

Abruptly the door flew open, banging against the wall as if the Atrox were impatient to welcome her. At once she felt its familiar tug. She stepped forward and was almost in the living room before she realized she had even moved.

She gasped. The Atrox stood in human form again, his arrogant face and piercing eyes more enticing than her memory of him, his unnatural strength and evil creating a dark aura of writhing shadow.

"Penelope." The Atrox called her by her old name, his voice brutal and at the same time alluring. "I've come to take back my gift."

"I surrender it easily," she said. "Your immortality was always a curse."

He touched her and a burst of silver sparks burst into the air. His fingers stole the warmth from her body, draining the power of the elixir.

At once she began to wrinkle, lines crinkling over her hands, veins becoming ropy under paper-thin skin. She could feel death's cold breath on her shoulder, but it didn't frighten her.

She closed her eyes, trying to bar the Atrox from her mind, and released her thoughts to warn the girl who would succeed her. But the Atrox seeped inside her, chasing after her telepathic message to see where she had sent it. Abruptly she stopped.

In anger the Atrox grasped her tighter, but she didn't feel the pain; death was pulling her into another realm.

She clasped the forbidden amulet, enjoying the fear in the Atrox's eyes. The talisman thrummed against her trembling fingers, eager for release. She looked down, almost blind now, her eyes covered by a veil of cataracts. Magically the letters brightened within the silver.

The Atrox gripped her neck with a strangling hold to stop her breath, but she spoke first. "Dingirmah."

The word exploded with fire, calling upon the One Exalted Deity in the universe. Her chest thundered with the sound.

Before the Atrox could fall back into darkness and escape, she said the second word. "Nimena."

The name boomed across the room, summoning forth the goddess of creation in an ancient, forgotten language. The physical force of its sound shook the walls.

The Atrox released her and she tumbled to the floor.

The third word roared from her mouth as if someone else had spoken it and burst into the air with blinding light, setting her on fire. She chanted the incantation as purifying white flames consumed her body. Dying, she prayed her invocation would destroy the Atrox.

Her heartbeat slowed and something let go. She rose above her apartment into the night. Death was nothing more than the separation of the body from the mind. Joy transported her and she embraced the white moonlight.

Don't miss the next

DAUGHTERS OF THE MOON book,

The prophecy

"KYLE?" THIS WAS all Catty needed. Now there was a witness.

"Hi, Catty." Kyle leaned against a bookcase, grinning. He had gone to La Brea High until he had been expelled. Now he went to Turney, but she still saw him at Planet Bang, hanging out with all his crazy friends and acting wild.

"What are you doing here?" she asked, ignoring his smirk.

"You're asking me?" He raised one eyebrow, trying hard not to laugh.

She hated his cocky atitude. Girls fell for his gorgeous looks, but he was also a magnet for trouble. Rumors had been going around school about him even before he had been forced to leave.

"I'm serious. Why are you here?" she asked again, her mind racing.

"You're prowling around where you don't belong and you want me to explain what I'm doing?" He brushed the shaggy hair from his eyes.

"You should have told me you were watching," she said.

"Because . . . ?" He tilted his head as if he were waiting for her to explain. When she didn't, he continued. "Because it's rude to watch someone steal a valuable piece of art? I apologize. I didn't know."

She rolled her eyes. "You don't understand—"

"Unlike you, I'm not looking for an explanation." He frowned. "Just put the manuscript back."

She stared at him in challenge. There was no way she was going to let go of the Scroll now, but why was Kyle so interested in it?

"You were going to steal the manuscript, weren't you?" Her eyes narrowed, watching him carefully.

"Do you think you're the only one a reporter hired to sneak in and get the scoop?" Kyle replied.

"That's why you're here?" Catty asked. His answer seemed possible, but she didn't believe him.

"I don't need this conversation." He started to walk away, but then his eyes caught something below her neck and he turned back.

She folded her arms over her breasts, a blush rising to her cheeks.

His hand shot out and she jerked back. "What are you doing?"

"Your necklace is shining." He gave her a curious look, then grabbed her moon charm.

"Ouch!" He let it go as if the metal had stung him. "What is it?"

Catty glanced down. Her amulet glowed in warning. Were Followers near? Or was there another reason she should be alert? She studied Kyle. Maybe he was a Follower and had planned to steal the Scroll as a way to prove himself worthy. He had a bad-boy reputation, but she had never sensed anything evil about him. There was only one way to know for sure. She clasped his fingers to see if her amulet had burned him. His hand was fine.

Before she could ask any more questions, approaching footsteps grew loud on the other side of the door.

His eyes shot up. "We have to hide." He eased back into the corner near the floor to ceiling bookshelves.

Catty ignored his outstretched hand. She had what she had come for, and now she was going to travel into the past.

Kyle lunged forward and grabbed her wrist. "Are you trying to get us caught?

Suddenly, Kyle was unzipping her backpack.

"Don't," she whispered, too late.

He pulled out the Scroll and set it on the table as the doornob turned.

She pitched forward, reaching for the manuscript. "You don't understand."

He caught her hand and yanked her back.

The door started to open. A slant of fluorescent light from the hallway fell across the carpet.

LYNNE EWING is a screenwriter who also counsels troubled teens. In addition to writing all of the books in the Daughters of the Moon series, she is the author of two ALA Quick Picks: *Drive-By* and *Party Girl.* Ms. Ewing lives in Los Angeles, California.